The Crystal Pelican

Gregory Payette

8 Flags Publishing, Inc.

Sign up for the newsletter on my website:

GregoryPayette.com

Once or twice a month I'll send you updates and news. Plus, you'll be the first to hear about new releases with special prices. If you'd like to receive the Henry Walsh prequel (for free) use the sign-up form here: **GregoryPayette.com/crossroad**

Chapter 1

ALEX LOOKED DOWN AT my bags on the floor behind me. "So where are you going to sleep?"

"Tonight?" I shrugged as I sipped my Guinness. "Billy said I could sleep on the couch in his office."

"Upstairs?" Alex cringed. "Have you seen that couch? Don't let your bare skin come in contact with it."

I finished my beer and slid the empty pint toward the edge of the bar.

The bartender, Chloe, looked my way and I held up two fingers. "Two more...one for Alex."

Chloe gave me a nod and brought two Guinness pints. I grabbed mine before it touched the bar. She put the other down in front of Alex.

I turned to Alex. "Would've been nice if Philip had at least given me a little more of a heads-up he'd be taking back his boat."

"Didn't you say they're going back to Australia after their wedding?"

"That's what he said. But the wedding's a month away. Although I shouldn't complain...I enjoyed my life on a boat for a few years."

"And you didn't have to pay for it."

Alex was a good friend and the Associate Director of Security when we both worked for the Jacksonville Sharks baseball team. After I left to start my own private investigations business, Alex took over as Director, but helped me out with my cases whenever she could.

"It's only been a few hours, and I already miss being on the boat," I said. "There's nothing like it. You wake up in the morning and all you hear is the river and a few birds. It's hard to come back and live on land like the rest of you humans."

Alex looked down at my half empty glass. "You've had a lot to drink," she said. "You sure you're okay?"

I shook my head. "No, I'm not okay. And I'm thirsty." I looked toward Chloe and gestured to bring us two more.

Alex waved her off as she pointed down to the Guinness she'd barely touched. "I'm all set." She took a sip from her glass and turned to me. "Are you trying to get me drunk?"

I held the glass under my mouth and shook my head. "I'm trying to get me drunk. And I don't feel like doing it alone today."

She gave me a look. "Well, I can't sit around drinking all day. Some of us have things to do."

"Like what?"

She didn't answer.

"If I had a place to go maybe I'd leave."

"Well, if you decide to pass on that skanky couch upstairs, you know my door's always open. The bedroom on the first floor is all yours."

Chloe put another pint down in front of me. "Thanks Chloe." I looked straight ahead toward the TV on the backside of the bar. I leaned into Alex "You don't want me staying at your house. It'd be dangerous."

She cracked half a smile. "Dangerous?"

I straightened myself up in my seat. "Philip could decide to stay on the boat, even after the wedding. Or maybe he'll sell it. Who knows...I have no idea what his plans are. And you might never get rid of me."

Chloe put two shot glasses down on the bar and gave us each a good pour of Jack Daniels.

Alex looked at her watch. "I can't do this right now."

I pushed one of the shot glasses a little closer to her and raised mine up in a toast. "To being homeless," I said as I threw the shot straight down my throat.

Alex took her time and sipped hers. "You know I don't drink this stuff."

I wiped my mouth with the back of my hand and pushed the empty glass toward the edge of the bar. "By the way, Philip told me to bring a guest."

"To what, his wedding?"

I nodded. "I told him I might."

Alex finished her shot of Jack and chased it with the full glass of Guinness in front of her. I thought she knew where I was going but didn't say a word.

I said, "I thought maybe you'd want to come with me? Should be nice. It's at the Timuquana Country Club."

"When?"

"End of the month. The twenty ninth."

She looked down at her phone. "That's a Monday."

"Oh, okay. Then it's the twenty-seventh."

She shrugged. "Why not? But if I meet one of his wealthy friends, don't get upset if I disappear with him."

I leaned on the bar, my arms folded in front of me.

Alex looked at the thick, black diver's watch on her wrist. "I really do have to go."

"I don't think you should drive," I said. "You can have the couch upstairs...I'll sleep in the chair."

"I'll do Uber."

"Then you might as well have another." I held up two fingers to Chloe.

I reached my hand into my pocket and pulled out my phone. I took a quick look at the screen and put it away. "A potential client was supposed to call tonight." I leaned back in the stool, my arms crossed in front of me. "Not as easy as I thought it'd be, being out on my own chasing clients."

I could feel Alex watching me. She said, "You regret turning down that offer with the sheriff's office?"

"A steady check wouldn't have been bad. And, of course, you've made it clear you only want a man with money... "

Alex gave me a look. "I don't know of anyone who gets rich working for the sheriff."

Chloe put two more shots down in front of me and Alex.

I threw mine back, finished my Guinness, and slid the glass across the bar. Alex let the full shot of Jack sit there in front of her. "I can't do it. Seriously, I'm—"

I grabbed her shot and finished it myself. "I'm going to go take a look upstairs. Make sure I want to throw down my stake before Billy gets back. I'd hate to insult him, decline his offer." I stood from the stool and reached down for my bags. I tossed one over each shoulder. "You want to come up and check it out?"

Alex shook her head, tapping on her phone. "Uber's on the way. And I'm not sure my shots are up-to-date."

"You're leaving?"

She nodded. "You get itchy from that couch, call me. I'll have the room ready, just in case." Alex waved goodbye to Chloe. I stood and watched her walk away. Before she got to the door, she turned and said, "Call me later."

Chapter 2

I OPENED MY EYES with my face smashed into the cushion of the couch in Billy's office. A foul odor was embedded in the fabric I hadn't noticed with all the drinks in me from the night before.

My head pounded. My neck was so sore, I could barely turn to see the clock on the wall. There were no blinds or shades on the windows but it didn't matter. It was dark outside.

I reached down to the floor and grabbed my watch from my pants pocket. I squinted and tried to clear the blur so I could see the time.

Four in the morning.

Even when I was a kid I woke up earlier than everyone else in the house. I'd wake up anxious, like I was afraid of missing something or was wasting time staying in bed. Over the years I grew to appreciate the quiet in the earliest part of the day.

I got dressed and left Billy's, then walked alone along the road toward Trout River Marina, the place I'd lived on the boat for the past few years.

The truth was, I'd had a pretty nice life there. And I enjoyed my life on the boat owned by my friend, Philip Wetzel.

But Philip showed up with his new fiancé and told me he wanted to spend some time on his boat. It was, after all, his boat to take back. I was nothing more than a temporary guest taking care of it for him while he traveled the world with his beautiful fiancé, Victoria Collins. He didn't think twice when he said they both thought it would be fun to "rough it" and stay on the boat.

I continued down Trout River Drive, looked down at my sneakers and—for a split second—thought maybe I'd pick up the pace and turn my casual walk into a run. But that thought didn't last long.

Inside the gate of the marina I stood and looked toward the boats docked along the edge of the St. Johns. The yellow light from the lamp posts brightened the parking lot. Red and orange started to fill the sky as the sun worked its way above the horizon. There was no noise, other than the river and idling boats and fishermen trying to get out ahead of the hot, Florida sun.

I missed it already.

"Henry?"

Philip was standing behind me, breathing heavily. Sweat poured down his face. He wore running shoes and shorts but no shirt, showing off his thin, sculpted body with his six pack abs. "What are you doing over here?" he said. He cracked a crooked smile. "You forget we were staying on the boat?"

I shook my head. "Just out for a morning walk...sort of ended up over here. A habit, I guess."

Philip wiped his forehead with the back of his arm. "I've been meaning to talk to you about that," he said. "Won't be long until we're off, married, heading back to Australia. I don't know how long we'll be gone." He turned and looked behind us, facing east where the sun was trying to break the horizon. "Maybe one day I can persuade Victoria to move back to the States. I don't know what your plans are, and if you'd still want to take care of the boat once we leave?"

I knew Philip didn't seem to care whether or not I had a place to stay. He just wanted to make sure his boat would be taken care of.

"I'm looking at some options right now," I said. "I'll let you know, though. I've been thinking about getting a place on the beach. If I hadn't grown up in Fernandina Beach, I'd—"

"I thought you loved this place?" Philip said as he looked ahead toward the river. "You seem to be pretty popular around here."

"Let me think about it, okay? It's just ... I need some stability in my life."

Philip tilted his head to the side. "Stability? You have all this ... stability would be the last thing I would worry about if I were you." He shrugged. "But you let me know. If not, I'll have to find someone else." He started to walk away and waved his hand for me to follow him. "Why don't you come have a coffee at the boat?"

I laughed. "Not if you're using that old Mr. Coffee down in the galley. Picked that up at a yard sale. I only use it when I'm desperate for a caffeine kick or the kitchen at the restaurant's closed."

Philip said, "That thing? We threw that out, bought an espresso machine."

I walked with Philip along the dock toward the boat, a walk I'd made hundreds of times over the past few years. But for some reason I felt uncomfortable and out of place.

Philip said, "Victoria was asleep when I left for my run. Hopefully she's up now. She'll be delighted to see you."

Delighted, I thought. A word I don't think has ever come out of my mouth. It's reserved for people like Philip—when they remove the silver spoon at birth they teach you to say words like delighted.

"Don't wake her up on my account," I said. "It's early."

Philip walked ahead of me. "She'd normally try to run with me, but complains she can't keep up. I try to run five miles. Then maybe take out the bike when I can." He slapped himself in the belly. "Gotta stay in shape as we age." He looked me up and down. "You don't exercise?"

I put my hand on my stomach and sucked it in, but didn't say a word.

He stepped up onto the boat and leaned over the ladder for the cabin down below. "Victoria," he said. He repeated her name. "Victoria? Are you awake? Henry Walsh is here, wants to say hello." He turned, looked at me and shrugged. He stepped down the ladder and disappeared into the cabin.

His head popped up the hole as he climbed back up the ladder. "She's not here."

"You sure she's not in the head?" I said.

He didn't answer.

I said, "Maybe she went for a run?"

"No. She pulled her Achilles. That's why she didn't come with me this morning. The doctor told her to take some time off. She wants to be sure she'll be able to move all right for the wedding."

Philip rubbed the side of his boyish face with his open hand. He turned, glanced toward Jed's, the marina's restaurant. "Maybe she went to get something to eat."

"They're not open yet," I said.

He looked at me, but said nothing. He turned and stepped back down into the cabin below.

I raised my voice so he could hear me down below. "Your car here?"

He didn't answer.

I walked along the dock and stepped up onto the boat. I looked down into the river, although I made sure Philip didn't notice.

I was looking for Victoria.

He came up with his keys in his hands. "The keys to my car were down below."

"You try her phone?"

He nodded. But pulled his phone from his pocket anyway, tapped the screen and put it up to his ear.

He shook his head, "It went right to voicemail." He started to put his phone back in his pocket when it rang. He answered, "Victoria?" Quiet for a moment, he said, "Where are you?" His eyes were on me now, the phone up to his ear. His mouth was open, as if ready to speak, but he said nothing.

After thirty-seconds his arm dropped down below his side, still holding onto the phone. "It's Victoria."

"What'd she say?"

He slowly shook his head with a dazed look in his eyes. He looked out toward the water. In a quiet, almost hushed voice, he looked up at me and said, "She's being held. Someone is demanding one million dollars if I want to see her again."

I reached down for the phone in his hand and took it from him. "What's your password?"

He didn't answer.

"Philip, look at me. What's your password?"

He lifted his eyes. "Six-four-eight-three."

"Was it her phone?"

He shook his head.

I tapped on the number that'd called him and called it back. It rang three or four times. Nobody answered.

A message came on:

The user at this number cannot be reached. Please try again later.

The call disconnected.

"What is it?" Philip said.

I gave him his phone. "Call the sheriff's office."

He shook his head. "She said if I call the police she'd be killed."

I rubbed my forehead, turning and looking all around the marina.

"What else did she say?"

Philip looked me in the eye. "You have to help me, Henry."

"What else did they say?"

"I should expect another call with further instructions."

Chapter 3

PHILIP STAYED CLOSE TO the boat as he clutched his phone tight in his hand. He paced back-and-forth along the dock. I walked over to Jed's —the restaurant at the marina—and hoped somebody might've seen something or somebody come into the marina.

The problem was they weren't open that early in the morning. The only people in there at the time were the restaurant's owners, Margaret and Ronnie. And neither had seen a thing.

Ronnie said, "I'm barely awake that early in the morning. But even still, we were both in the back kitchen, not paying much attention to what was going on outside."

I walked across the lot toward the front of the entrance to the marina. I'd already called Alex and she was on her way over. It'd been a day off for her—one of many—since she'd been let go as Security Director with the Jacksonville Sharks baseball team.

After the team owner Bob Campbell had sold the team a year earlier, Alex stayed on in my old position as Director of Security. But she was let go by the new owners who decided to outsource their security staff to Bishop Security. She'd been out of work ever since, even though Andrew Bishop, the CEO of Bishop Security, had offered her a position with his company.

So she'd had some time on her hands and helped me out when she could. Most of the work I'd had involved following cheating spouses. I just wasn't busy enough for her to help full time.

I spotted Alex's yellow Jeep along Trout River Drive. She pulled into the parking lot and stopped next to me, the engine still running. "Any word?"

I shook my head.

"What'd they say?" she said.

"Whoever it is wants a million dollars, or Philip will never see her again."

Alex stared back at me. "I assume he has it?"

"I didn't ask, but I'm sure if he doesn't he can get his hands on it." I turned and looked toward Philip's boat. "He's afraid to leave the area. He's waiting for the call back."

I gave a nod toward a parking spot on the other side of her Jeep. "Park there, we'll walk over to the boat."

"Where's your car?"

"I actually walked here this morning."

Alex pulled her Jeep into the parking space as a black Chevy Suburban with dark, tinted windows drove past me, a few feet from where I was standing. Even the windshield was tinted, too dark for me to see the driver. I kept my eye on the vehicle as it passed me then turned onto Trout River Drive and disappeared out of sight.

Alex stepped out of her Jeep.

"You see that Suburban?" I said, looking toward the street.

She shook her head, looking around the lot. "Where?"

"Just drove past us." I pulled my sunglasses down over my eyes.

I turned and headed back toward Philip's boat. I didn't see him out on the dock, where he'd just been standing a moment before. I started to pick up my pace.

Alex caught up and walked alongside me.

I looked at her. "We need to help him find Victoria. But until whoever it is calls Philip back, we're at a standstill."

Alex said, "I know she said not to, but don't you think we should call the sheriff's office?"

I glanced at her and hurried toward the boat. "We'll wait for the call back. If they were going to do anything to her they wouldn't have called in the first place. I'm hoping if we get what they asked for, she'll stay safe."

We were no more than fifty yards away, I pulled out my phone and called Philip's cell. I didn't see him anywhere. It rang once. He didn't answer. Second ring, nothing. Third ring...

A light flashed across the marina, followed by a deafening explosion that shook the ground under our feet and knocked us both down to the ground. We looked toward Philip's boat from our backs, where thick, black smoke poured from the raging fire coming up from the water where Philip's boat had been docked moments before.

Alex had blood dripping down her arm.

"You're bleeding." I said.

She nodded. "I'm okay."

I didn't know if I was okay or not. I could barely hear. When Alex spoke her voice was muffled, like she'd spoken from inside a box. My hands were scraped and bloodied.

I ran toward the boat with Alex right behind me.

As we approached the dock, I stopped and put my arm out across her chest like a mother does to her child when stopping short in a car. "Wait," I said. "Stay here."

She pushed my arm away and walked with me toward the dock. There was little left to Philip's boat, although it was still there, pieces of it floating in the river

I yelled for him, but could barely hear my own voice. My ears were ringing.

Scraps of smoldering wood and fiberglass and pieces of metal covered the docks and some of the surrounding boats.

I turned to Alex. "He was on that boat..."

I looked down toward the water. The volume from screams around us started to grow as my hearing slowly returned.

Dozens of people—fisherman and liveaboards and Ronnie from the restaurant—ran toward the docks. Ronnie's wife Margaret stood, staring toward the water with her mouth covered with both hands.

I scanned the parking lot, the heat and glow from the burning fire to my back. Philip's car was still parked where he'd left it. But there was no sign of him anywhere.

Ronnie moved past me and pulled a garden hose behind him. I helped him pull it closer to the boat. But it did little to ease the flames. Others grabbed buckets and tossed water on the docks to slow the spread of fire until Jacksonville Fire and Rescue showed up.

I looked around and yelled over the roaring fire, "Everyone! We need to back off."

Margaret walked up behind me, tears in her eyes. "I was afraid that it was you in there, Henry."

I looked down on the ground and spotted a blackened, smoldering cell phone. I kneeled down and used the edge of my shirt to pick it up without burning my fingers. The glass was shattered. There was a charred but clear cover on the back with what was left of a photo tucked behind it.

The photo was of Victoria.

The sirens screamed as fire trucks and Sheriff's vehicles pulled into Trout River Marina. Dozens of firemen and medics ran full speed pulling the hoses and carrying equipment from their trucks.

One of the firemen on the dock turned and yelled to everyone in the area. "Get away from the boat!"

We all turned and ran for cover. Most of us ducked behind one of the firetrucks as the boat exploded once again. Flames shot high into the sky and smoke poured from what was left of Philip's boat, which seemed to be nothing more than smoldering pieces of burning debris that littered the St. Johns River.

I couldn't help but believe Philip was dead.

Chapter 4

Divers from the sheriff's office and Jacksonville Fire and Rescue Department Thirty-Four were down in the water just off the docks, in the precise location where I'd lived on Philip's boat for nearly three years.

There was little left to the boat itself once the fire was finally extinguished.

Mike Stone, a veteran detective with the Jacksonville Sheriff's Department took a drag from his cigarette and glanced at me as he inhaled. He let out a stream of smoke just past my head and gave me a stare. "Not surprised to see you involved here, Walsh." He tossed the butt on the ground and rubbed it into the asphalt with the bottom of his shoe. He picked it up and tossed it underhand into a steel barrel a few feet away. "So tell me one more time. You used to live here, but you don't any longer? And that was your boat?"

I shook my head. "The owner is a friend of mine. I took care of it for him while he lived overseas. So, yes, I lived on it. But he'd come back recently, so I wasn't staying on it any longer."

He narrowed his eyes and looked toward the Fire and Rescue boat—part of the F and R's Marine Unit—just a few feet off the docks. He stuck another cigarette in his mouth and let it hang there without lighting it. It was a look I'm sure he got off the cop shows he watched just to perfect his tough-cop mannerisms.

Mike stepped toward the dock as the divers came up from the river. He said to one of the divers, "Any sign?"

The diver, a female, shook her head, pulled the mask from her face and walked away.

Mike turned and looked at Alex. "So what exactly were you two doing down here this early in the morning?"

I was about to answer myself, but Alex had a much better relationship with Mike than I did. So I kept my mouth shut.

"Henry was down here, out for a run."

Mike looked me up and down. "You? A run?" He let out a slight snort.

"I was out for a walk."

"Why here?" he said.

"Why here, what?"

"Why walk here? You said you don't live here anymore, but you came here anyway?"

I looked him right in the eye but didn't answer.

He gave Alex a look, cupped his hands over his cigarette and lit it. He turned back to me. "Where'd you walk from?"

"Why's that matter?"

Mike took a drag from his cigarette. "If it didn't matter I wouldn't have asked." He held his glare at me and exhaled his smoke, again, toward my face.

"I'm staying upstairs from Billy's Place."

He gave me a smirk. "That's where you live?"

I turned and walked away from him.

18

"Hey, I'm not done with you," he said.

But I ignored him, standing a few feet away looking toward the water and close enough to hear Alex and Mike.

Alex said, "Why are you treating him like some kind of suspect?"

Mike turned his head to me and raised his voice. "Am I treating you like a suspect, Henry?"

I turned and looked at him over my shoulder, without answering.

Mike stepped toward me. "Listen, you don't have to take everything so personally. Am I a little suspicious you're here? Yes. It's clear you must know something. And I know the alleged victim is a friend of yours...even though he tossed you off his boat so he'd have a good night's sleep. Is that right?"

I turned a little, looked at him and nodded.

Alex walked ahead of us and leaned over the edge of the dock, her gaze toward the water.

Mike scratched his head. "Was Philip here alone?"

Alex bent down and picked something up off the dock. She turned and looked back at me and Mike.

"I don't know. He had a girlfriend. A fiancé."

Mike's smug expression dropped from his face. As if talking to himself, he said, "There could've been a second victim." He squinted, again scratching his head as he took a drag of his cigarette. "Was she on that boat?"

I shook my head.

"But she's here? In town?"

"She might be. I'm not sure." I glanced at Alex. She had her back to us, looking out toward the river.

19

Mike walked away without saying another word, stopping to talk to a group of the men and women standing on the dock in diving gear.

• • • ● • ● • • •

Alex and I stood by her Jeep. "You don't think you should tell Mike about Victoria?"

I shook my head and shrugged. "I honestly don't know. But I didn't lie. I don't know if Victoria was on that boat. As far as I know, she wasn't." I stepped up into her Jeep, grabbed the roll bar over my head and sat down in the passenger seat. "I tell him about the call, then what? She told Philip not to call the sheriff's office. Mike gets involved, then what? They kill her? It's all on me."

"What if something happens to her and you didn't tell them?"

I looked out the side view mirror toward the docks. "I don't know what I'm supposed to do. Not a lot of options right now." I pulled Philip's charred phone from my pocket and looked at it, front-and-back. "Know anyone who can get this phone to work?"

Alex said, "You took evidence from the scene?"

I looked her right in the eye and paused for a moment. "Can you get it to work?"

She turned the key, started the Jeep, and took the phone from my hand. She looked at both sides of it, then tucked it in the storage box between our seats. "I'll see what I can do."

"See if we can get some numbers from it." I could tell, watching Alex, her wheels were turning. "What're you thinking?" I said.

She shrugged her shoulders. "If Victoria was really kidnapped..."

I cocked my head. "Why should we think she wasn't?"

"Well..." She hesitated. "It's just that Philip gets this alleged phone call, early in the morning, right? But how do they come and take her off the boat? Who would've known Philip wasn't there? That he'd gone out for a run that early?"

Alex turned the steering wheel, maneuvered the Jeep around the Sheriff's vehicles and Jacksonville Fire and Rescue vehicles. TV trucks took what little space was left in the marina's parking lot.

"You know, something crossed my mind...I know this sounds a little crazy but what if that bomb was for me?"

Alex said, "Well, technically they're not sure it was a bomb. But, either way...why would you say that?"

"I don't know. I have my enemies, you know. And a lot of them might know I used to live on that boat."

• • • • ● • ● • • •

We were back at Alex's house and sat in the driveway, neither of us stepping down from the Jeep.

Alex said, "I still think you need to tell Mike everything you know."

"Why?"

"Because he's a detective. It's his job. It makes no sense for you to—"

"I know he's your friend," I said. "Or whatever you call him. But I can't help it. I don't trust they'll do the right thing. That means putting Victoria's life in danger."

"But two people are missing. Who knows, they both might be dead." Alex turned to me in her seat and tucked one leg up under the other. "You don't like Mike because he does everything by the book."

"No, I don't like him because he's got an ego the size of Texas."

She paused and looked straight ahead toward her house in front of where we were parked. She turned to me and said, "Henry, you know how they say that pilots, when they're flying a plane—"

"Hold on," I said. "What exactly do pilots flying a plane have to do with?"

Alex sighed. "Will you just listen to me for a second? Pilots are supposed to trust their instruments. Period. They're not trained to improvise unless it's the last resort. You don't fly with your gut."

"Okay," I said. "Thanks for the flying lesson."

She gave me a look. "Mike trusts his instruments. You go by your gut. There's a time and place for both. But you can't fault him for being the way he is. He's a good cop...a good detective."

"Great work when Jackie Lawson was falsely accused and ended up behind bars, wasn't it?"

Alex stared back at me, slowly shaking her head. She stepped from the Jeep and walked up the walkway to her house. Her dog, Raz, was waiting for her inside the door.

She turned and over her shoulder said, "You coming?"

I got out and walked toward her.

She stuck her key in the door and turned to me. "You and Mike would actually work well together. It's sort of a good fit. You know how they say opposites attract."

"I never believed that was true. Opposites are opposites for a reason."

She held the door open with her hip and I followed her inside, the temperature not much different from the warm outside air, although it was cooling a bit with a break in the season, but still warm.

"Is your AC broken?"

She threw her keys on the counter in the kitchen and kneeled down to pet her dog, Raz. "That whole house fan that came with the place does a good job, especially at night. Sucks the warm air right out the roof without running the HVAC unit." She stood up straight and opened the fridge. "Are you hungry?"

"I am. But I wonder if you're right. Maybe I should talk to Mike. If Philip's dead, there's a chance we'll never know who has Victoria."

Chapter 5

I MET MIKE STONE later in the afternoon at the Prairie Dog Pub, not far from the marina where the Trout River feeds into the St. Johns.

"Thanks for meeting me," I said and pulled out the stool next to him at the bar. "You haven't hauled me in so I assume that means I'm not on your suspect list?"

He turned to me without saying a word, then looked ahead and took a sip from his glass. "Alex said you had something to share with me. That's the only reason I'm here."

I ordered a Jack Daniels from the bartender. "Okay, well if we're going to be honest with each other. Then I might as well tell you...I wasn't completely up-front with you yesterday, at the marina."

Mike gave me a quick glance out of the corner of his eye, but kept his head faced forward. "I figured as much." He took another sip from his drink. "Hope you're not wasting my time. I got work to do, you know."

What a prick. I thought about not telling him a thing. Walk out, let him come after me. But Alex made me promise I'd tell him what I knew, let the sheriff's office do their job. "You asked me about Philip's girlfriend."

He turned to me and nodded. "Victoria Collins." His face got twisted a bit. "We don't think she was on the boat. No luck locating her just yet. It doesn't help that nobody seems to know who she is."

I waited a moment. "She's his fiancé, from Australia. She was on the boat with him earlier that morning, but not when I showed up."

Mike gave me a blank stare but didn't say a word.

I continued. "Philip got a call in the early morning while I was there. It was from Victoria, but she said she'd been abducted."

"Are you shitting me, Walsh?"

I shook my head. "I didn't want to put her at risk. Philip was told to pay a ransom."

"How much?"

"One million dollars. I didn't tell you because they told her to say if the cops were involved she'd be killed."

Mike rubbed his face with both hands. "Jesus Christ, Walsh." He shook his head. "So that explosion happened after he got the call that his girlfriend had been kidnapped?"

I nodded. "She was the one who called him."

"You do realize by not telling me this yesterday you're—"

"Mike." I turned in my seat, facing him. "I'm telling you now."

He finished what was in his glass and gave the bartender a nod. The bartender grabbed the bottle of Jim Beam and poured it over the ice in Mike's glass.

"Jim Beam, huh?"

Mike looked straight ahead and sipped off the top of his bourbon. Without facing me, he said, "They called his cell phone?"

"Yes."

"There was no phone found at the scene. Could be anywhere down along the river at this point."

I nodded, knowing Mike would take me in if I told him I'd taken a crucial piece of evidence from the scene. Alex was already having the data extracted from Philip's phone, and maybe I'd share what we found without telling him we had it. "We called the number back. It was a dead line. Either a burner phone or they re-routed the—"

"I know how it works." He shot back what was left in his glass and pushed it forward on the bar. He gave a nod with his chin to the bartender. "If there's anything else you're not telling me, I'll haul you down the station."

I pretended I didn't hear him, ignoring his threat. "There was an SUV in the parking lot that caught my eye."

The bartender poured another shot of Jim Beam into Mike's glass.

Mike said, "What SUV?"

"A big Suburban. Black, all the windows tinted. Got the plate." I reached into my pocket and pulled out a piece of paper with the plate number on it. I grabbed a cocktail napkin, wrote down the number and slid it to Mike.

Mike took the napkin, looked at it, and pushed it aside. "So, you saw a Suburban in the parking lot." He grabbed his glass and put it up to his mouth. Before he took a sip, over the glass he said, "Am I supposed to put out an APB to be on the lookout for an SUV you saw driving through a parking lot?"

"Just kind of stuck out. I know most of the cars that come through there."

He said, "You see anyone?"

"No. Windows were tinted real dark. And with the way the sun was rising, it reflected off the windshield when they drove by."

"Did Alex see it?"

"No."

Mike made a face, like he wanted to roll his eyes but in a much cooler, tough-cop way. He grabbed his glass and knocked back what was left in it. He got up from his stool, pulled a couple of bills from his pocket and stuck them under the empty glass. Without saying another word, he turned and headed for the door.

"Hey Mike, anything else you need just let me know."

He stopped, turned toward me with a cigarette in his mouth. "Stay out of the way. And don't keep anything else from me."

Chapter 6

BILLY TOLD ME TO give an old friend of his out in Yulee a call about a car he was selling on the cheap. But the thing I didn't realize was when Billy'd said old friend...he'd be a ninety-seven-year-old man who'd still been driving everywhere and every day. As his friend told me, he knew he was "on the clock" and wanted to purchase one last, brand new car.

So he bought a BMW Z4 convertible.

Billy's friend gave me quite a deal for what I considered my first luxury car. Aside from the fact it had one-hundred forty-seven-thousand miles on the odometer and it was just over thirteen years old, I had myself a new car.

New to me, of course.

Driving from the old man's house made me think about my parents; the inevitableness of time and what's at the end of the road for each of us.

Heading back to Jacksonville on Route 17 I picked up my phone and called them, just to check-in. As I dialed, I remembered the news was made for old people like my parents who sit around and watch a lot of TV. Especially the news.

As soon as he answered the phone, the first words out of my father's mouth was, "You hear about the explosion at the marina down there on the St. Johns?" I heard him whisper something to my mom, who must have been right there next to him. "That's not the same marina where you live, is it?"

"Actually, it is. But I hadn't been staying there. Philip—the guy who owns the boat—had been staying on it the past few days."

I could hear the nerves in my father's voice, cracking a bit more as his age crept up in years. "So you're okay?"

"I am. But I don't know if Philip is. He might've been on the boat when it exploded."

He said, "Where have you been staying?" It was as if he hadn't heard what I'd told him about Philip.

"You know Billy, right? I've been staying with him, upstairs from his restaurant."

There was a pause. "You're living upstairs from a restaurant?"

"It's temporary," I said. "Although Billy offered it to me to use as an office. I guess I'd sleep there, too."

"For your business?"

"Uh huh."

The line went quiet.

He said, "Are you doing okay, financially?"

I was hoping he didn't ask. "It's going okay. Takes a little while to get things moving."

"I remember when I started my first business. You were little. Some nights I didn't know if I could afford the grocery store on the way home."

I knew how that felt.

"So your friend, was he on the boat alone?"

"I don't know for sure if he was on the boat. But he'd had his fiancé with him. Her name's Victoria. It's... it's a long story. As far as we know, she wasn't on the boat. The truth is, I don't know where she is."

"She's missing?"

"I guess I can't really get into it as much as you'd like me to. The sheriff's office is involved, and I'm not exactly sure what's going on with any of this."

"Oh ..." I could hear the TV in the background. "Didn't you have a girlfriend named Victoria when you were up north?"

I didn't want to answer him. But Dad was the type who'd keep asking questions until he got the answers. I guess I know where I got it from. "I introduced them."

The truth was I'd met Victoria in Newport when I was working a detail up there during one of the Newport Bermuda races. We'd gone out a few times. She met Philip and they kind of hit it off.

"Is anybody looking for her?"

"Yes, of course, but—"

"What a situation you've gotten yourself into. You're living on the boat of the man who's dating your ex-girlfriend, then he takes the boat back?" He made a huffing noise. "And they were supposed to get married?"

"She wasn't ever my girlfriend. And, hopefully, they'll still be married...if I can find them." I desperately wanted to change the subject. "So how's Mom?" I said.

"You want to talk to her?"

"Yes, put her on."

There was some fumbling on the other end of the phone. Dad tried to fill mom in on some of the business we'd discussed.

Mom took the phone. "Henry? Is everything all right?"

"I'm fine. What about you, mom, is everything good?"

"Sure, everything's good. Your father and I are enjoying it out here on the west coast." She went quiet. "Did I hear dad say something about a girlfriend?"

I let out a laugh. "No, nothing about a girlfriend."

Mom was always wondering about the women in my life. Most of which she didn't have to know about, because they weren't in my life long enough to tell her.

"What about Alex?" she said. "Are you two—"

"No, mom. Alex is good, but we're just friends. We work together, that's all."

"What was dad saying about someone missing?"

"I'm working on a case...helping an old friend."

"I thought I heard him say someone's girlfriend is missing?" Mom always had good ears.

"Dad can tell you. But I need to get going so I can—"

"Henry?"

"Yes?"

"What are you doing for work now? Have you found another job yet?"

Mom worried about me. I guess like any mother she wanted her kid to settle down. Maybe stick with a nine-to-five...get married....have kids. "I own a business. I'm a private investigator."

"Okay, well, why don't you talk to your father..."

31

"Henry? Uh ... hold on, your mother's saying something." I heard his hand muffling the mouthpiece on the phone. "She wants to know when you're going to visit."

I felt a sense of guilt come over me. "I'll get out there soon. Sorry I haven't been out in a while."

My phone beeped and I looked at the screen. "Dad, I gotta grab this call. I'll call you again in a few days, okay?"

"Go ahead. Be safe, Henry."

I hung up and answered the other line—a number I didn't recognize. "Walsh Investigations." I didn't hear anyone on the other line. Again, I said, "Hello?"

After a moment of silence, I heard, "Henry? It's me."

"Philip?"

"Listen, I can't talk for long."

"You're alive?"

"Are you disappointed?"

"Jesus, Philip. Where are you?"

"I can't say right now. Not yet. But you have to help me."

"Of course. But you have to tell me—"

"I'll call you again. In another hour. We can meet, but I'll have to let you know where. It'll be late, sometime after dark."

I said, "Can't you tell me what's going on? Are you hiding?"

"I'll call you. Make sure you answer my call. It might be from a different number."

"What about Victoria? Is she..." The other end of the call was quiet. "Philip?"

He'd hung up.

My phone rang a few seconds later.

I answered without looking at the screen. "Walsh Investigations."

"Henry?"

"Dad, hey, sorry about that. I was just—"

He said, "Is everything okay?"

I paused for a moment after I repeated his question in my head.

'Is everything okay?'

I said, "I don't know. But I'm going to have to call you back later. Maybe tomorrow. I need to take care of something."

"Sure, I understand. Just be careful, okay?"

Before they moved to the west coast of Florida, Dad ran a business in Fernandina Beach repairing watches and clocks and some small electronics. He made a decent living without having to work for someone else, which I see wasn't such a bad goal...now that I'm a little older. He wanted me to jump into the business but also knew it wasn't what I wanted to do.

I needed action and a little adventure. Not necessarily boats blowing up in my face or missing friends...or the part about living on another friend's couch, not knowing where my next check would come from. Maybe it wasn't what I'd imagined when I was a kid watching Magnum PI. But it paid the bills.

Sometimes.

Chapter 7

ALEX WAS ALREADY AT the bar at Billy's Place when I walked down from the office with the couch I'd been sleeping on upstairs.

Billy had offered to let me use the upstairs as a place to sleep and work. Since he'd already built another office outside, off the back of the restaurant, we both agreed it'd be a shame to let the upstairs go to waste.

I had a nice view of the St. Johns River. And, best of all, rent was cheap.

Alex leaned over her plate at the bar and took a bite of the vegan wrap Billy had added to his menu, just for her. "You sure it was Philip?" she said after I told her about the phone call I'd received.

"Of course I'm sure. Why wouldn't it've been him?"

Alex looked at me, then swallowed as she wiped the edge of her mouth with her napkin. "Maybe someone's trying to lure you in. You're the one who said maybe it was for you. I'm just saying...you need to be careful"

Billy put a beer down on the bar in front of me.

I turned to Alex and said, "I don't want to let Mike know about it, either. Not until I know more."

"Mike's already asking a lot of questions. Said you just happened to forget to mention the SUV until he pulled it out of you."

"Pulled it out of me?" I laughed, shaking my head. "He's a tough guy when he retells his stories."

"Right now there are divers down in the river trying to find Philip. They're putting their lives in danger. To me, that's a big deal, Henry. So if you know where he is, I'm telling you right now, you need to—"

"Jesus, Alex. I don't know what kind of danger Philip's in. I mean, I appreciate you looking out for the sheriff's office, but if we tell Mike or anyone else over there, there's a good chance Philip'll disappear for good."

Billy stood in front of us, wiped a glass dry with his towel. "Is he hiding?"

I shrugged. "I don't know. He said he'd call me back." I turned away and looked toward the dining area. The crowd had picked up.

Alex took another bite from her wrap and tapped me on the arm. She held her finger up in the air, gesturing for me to wait. She swallowed then wiped her mouth again with her napkin. "I'm sorry, I haven't eaten all day. And I didn't sleep. My mind's—"

"Alex, I get it. Believe me. I don't like this anymore than you do. But this is real. I don't even know if I'm prepared to deal with this. And here I was, complaining about chasing the cheating husbands."

Alex's phone rang. She stood up from the bar and walked a few feet away to take the call.

A moment later she stepped back to the bar. "That SUV you saw at the lot. Turned out to be rented from a place called Darcy Car Rental."

"Who?"

"Darcy Car Rental."

"Never heard of it," I said.

Billy walked past us with dirty dishes in his hands and put them in a bin below the bar. "Never heard of what?"

I looked up at him. "Darcy Car Rental. That SUV I saw at the marina was rented from there."

"I know that place."

"Yeah?"

"It's one of those businesses people know about somehow but doesn't do any advertising. Might be a little shady, but I'm not sure." Billy looked at Alex. "Maybe someone's from out of town, wants to lay low...maybe with a girlfriend or just up to no good. You know what I mean? You rent from a hole-in-the-wall like Darcy Car Rental."

I said, "Or you have something in your background that prevents you from renting from a more established place. Or you want to pay with cash. Probably don't even need a driver's license."

• • • ● • ● • • •

I left Billy's Place, pulled down my sunglasses and walked to my car parked in the back lot. I saw a man standing near my car. He was wearing a baseball hat and sunglasses. I thought, for a moment, it was Philip.

But I got close enough and realized it wasn't. I didn't know who it was.

I stepped to the driver's side door of my Lexus and pulled on the handle as I looked across the top of my roof.

The man stood on the other side, staring back at me.

I said, "Sorry, no taxi service today." I stared back at him. "Is there something I can help you with?"

That's when he raised his hand over the roof, my eye looking straight into the muzzle of what looked to be a 9mm.

"Get in the car," the man said. He waved his gun with a slight flip of his wrist.

I looked back toward the entrance to Billy's Place and hoped Alex—normally armed with a Glock—might walk out the door. But I knew she'd planned to go upstairs to my office and do some research on the computer.

The problem was I wasn't in much of a position to argue with this man and his gun. So I did as he said and stepped into my car.

He kept his gun pointed at me from outside the window. I clicked the button and unlocked his door. When he stepped inside, he removed his sunglasses and his baseball cap and again flipped his gun back and forth. "Drive."

I had my hands on the steering wheel. "Where to?"

He didn't answer. There was something about him I recognized. Maybe his eyes. Of course I wondered if this guy had something to do with the explosion or with Philip or Victoria. Or if, as I couldn't help but think, this was all meant for me.

I pulled out of the parking lot, drove a mile or so and turned onto the Main Street Bridge. "Are you going to tell me what this is all about?"

"Shut up and drive."

I turned to him, slowly, as it hit me who he was. "Wait a minute. I know who you are." I thought for a moment. "I knew you looked like Philip." I looked down at his big stomach. "But he's in much better shape."

The gun still on me, he didn't respond.

"I remember meeting you. You were with Philip, in Newport. But that was a long time ago." I turned to him again. "You don't look like you've taken very good care of yourself."

"You might want to knock it off, Henry. I'm the one holding the gun."

I said, "Yeah, about that. Would you mind telling me what this is all about?"

"Where is he?"

"Where is who?"

I could hear him take a deep breath. "Don't play me for a fool, Henry. I'm telling you right now," he flicked his wrist with the gun in his hand, pointed right at me. "I'm not afraid to use this."

I glanced at him and shook my head. "Can you tell me where we're going?"

I noticed he wasn't wearing a seatbelt. And it crossed my mind to bash the car head-on into a wall of some sort. But I'd barely had the car for twenty-four hours and didn't need to wreck another car.

"Listen," I said. "I don't know if your brother's alive. I'm guessing you've heard about the explosion?"

"Just tell me where he is."

I turned to him. "How the hell would *I* know where he is? As far as I know, he didn't survive the explosion."

"Don't try to tell me he didn't survive. I know he's alive."

I said, "Frank, right? That's your name... Frank. It's coming back to me now." I took a quick look at his head. "I don't remember you being bald."

Frank pinched his lips, his face turning red. He racked the slide on his 9mm. "If you're helping him hide ..." He lifted his pistol, the muzzle inches from my face.

"Frank, listen. I'm telling you the truth. And what makes you think I'd have anything to do with any of this anyway?"

"Because I know you were there."

"Oh yeah?" I shot him a quick glance from the corner of my eye. "So then I assume that means you were there, too?"

Frank didn't answer.

"I don't get the feeling you're looking for him because you miss your younger brother."

"Younger brother? He's older than me. By five years."

I gave him another look, my gaze on his big stomach hanging over his waist.

"So if he is still alive, what is it you're looking for? Or are you just hoping to make sure if the explosion didn't get him, that gun in your hand will?"

Frank had yet to tell me where to go. I got the feeling he had no idea anyway. I turned off 95 to Main Street North. That's when I ripped the wheel down Busch Drive, my car almost on two wheels when I took the corner.

He smashed into the passenger-side door. I slammed on the brakes and his head bounced off the dashboard. His gun flew from his grip, bounced off the seat and landed on the floor. I slammed my foot on the gas and the gun slid under the seat.

He turned to me with a blank look in his eyes. He was dazed, blood coming down from his head. I reached for him, grabbed the side of his neck and pushed him toward the door. His hand moved around the floor as he tried to feel around for his gun.

With my knee holding the wheel steady, I used my left hand to reach across him and pull on the door handle. My other hand pushed against his neck, both of us struggling while the car was nearly going out of control.

I managed to get the passenger door open and pushed him out. We were moving at a pretty good clip and I watched him through my rearview mirror as he rolled and tumbled along the pavement and into the curb. I slowed for a moment, and he looked to be trying to get to his feet but he stumbled, falling to the ground.

I pulled my car to the curb, turned and watched out the rear window as Frank pushed himself up on one knee.

Knowing he wasn't dead, I slammed the pedal down to the floor and disappeared, leaving Frank—as they say—in the dust.

Chapter 8

PHILIP CALLED ME IN the early evening the next day and had me meet him at a kid's baseball park out in Yulee.

The parking lot was full, jammed with cars and parents and little kids in baggy baseball uniforms running between the parked cars. I couldn't remember the last time I'd been to Yulee field, but knew I'd played there as a kid.

I didn't know why Philip wanted me to meet at this particular field, other than it was a busy place and easy for us to hide.

He said he'd be parked under the sign at the entrance, but the only spot I could find was on the opposite end of the parking lot. I waited while a woman backed out in her minivan, kids screaming in the back. I watched as she nearly swiped the car next to her and screamed at her kids inside. It didn't help she had a phone in one hand, the steering wheel in the other.

I walked across the lot toward the sign where Philip said he'd be. A thin man with a thick beard, baseball cap and sunglasses looked my way. I got the feeling he was watching me, and I wondered if it was Philip.

I waited before I spoke up, just to be sure. The man walked toward me and as we were about to pass each other in the parking lot, he grabbed me by the arm.

"Henry." He pulled his glasses down onto his nose and looked me in the eye, then pushed his glasses back against his face. It was Philip. "Follow me."

I walked behind him. He glanced at me over his shoulder and gave a nod with his chin toward an older, green Chevy Impala. He unlocked the doors. "Get in."

"Nice car," I said.

"It's all I could get with the cash I had in my pocket."

I looked at him for a moment. With the fake beard, the sunglasses and hat he looked like Forest Gump did when he ran around the country. "Are you going to tell me what's going on?" I said.

Philip started the car and put it in drive, but didn't answer.

"Your brother Frank showed up," I said. "He pulled a gun on me, wanted to know where you were."

"He didn't believe I was dead?"

I said, "Apparently not."

Philip watched the road, and after a couple of miles he pulled down a dirt road, turned the car around to face the way we drove in, and put the car in park.

"I haven't heard from Frank in five years. Shows up now when somebody's trying to kill me."

"You think he'd have anything to do with it?"

Philip shrugged. "How'd you know Frank?"

"We met that time in Newport," I said. "Around the same time you met Victoria."

"Did he say what he wanted?"

"Somehow he knew I was at Billy's Place and followed me to my car. Had a gun, made me drive him around but never said where we were going. Like I said, he knew you were alive. And he was sure I knew where you were."

Philip was quiet, thinking. "How would he know?"

"That you were alive? It's a good question."

Philip said, "I didn't think he meant it when he threatened me."

"He threatened you?" I said. "Recently?"

Philip turned, looked out the driver side window. "He's not all there, if you know what I mean."

"I found your phone on the dock. Alex is trying to see what she can come up with, somehow hopefully we can track down the caller. Although I'm afraid they called on a burner phone, so..."

He said, "Did you ask him if he knew where she was? If he tried to kill me, who says he wouldn't kill her?"

I said, "You really think he'd kidnap his own brother's fiancé for a million dollars?"

Philip didn't answer, looking at me with his sunglasses off. His eyes were red and looked tired. He started the car and pulled ahead, turning toward the road.

I said, "I was looking for you, you know. Lucky for me I didn't make it onto the boat."

"I was going through Victoria's bags," he said. "I found a bag I didn't recognize... although she had so many of them. When I opened it," he glanced at me, then paused. "I looked inside and saw the device. I'd never seen a bomb before, outside of the movies. But when it hit me that's what it was, I dropped the bag and whatever else I had in my hand and ran up the ladder, up onto the deck. I was in such a panic, I tripped before I made it out and fell overboard into the water, then swam as fast as I could to get away. I was looking for a way up onto the dock, but there was nothing to grab onto. I spotted a dingy, swam to it and climbed up...paddling away from the boat."

I looked out the passenger window for a moment then turned to him. "Are you going to tell me why you're hiding?"

Philip looked at me with a crooked grin. "Isn't it obvious? Somebody wants me dead."

We drove under Route 95 and headed west on 200.

"But what if that bomb wasn't for you?" I said.

Philip stared straight ahead, watching the road. He turned to me and seemed to hesitate a moment. He sighed. "There are people who want something I at one time had in my possession. The problem is, they don't know I don't have it anymore."

"Like what?"

He nodded. "It's a piece of art. And it's made of a rare crystal. The rarest crystal on earth." He reached for the panel on the dash and adjusted the AC. "I don't know how much you know about my family, and where we got most of our wealth."

"Jewelry?"

He nodded. "Gems. My family was in the business of dealing rare gems. At one time we manufactured crystal figurines and sculptures. Some of these figures—even the tiniest of figurines—were worth thousands of dollars a piece. But that was just the tip of the iceberg. We started dealing with artists—sculpture artists—and realized when you combine art with a rare gem or, in this case, this particular grade of crystal, the value could be worth hundreds of thousands of dollars.

There are a few—two or three throughout the world—that have sold for millions. My father developed somewhat of a side business built around these artists and their sculptures."

"And one of the sculptures is missing?"

Again, he didn't answer, turning the wheel. "I don't care about that sculpture. Others do, of course. Enough to take Victoria and demand the money."

"Then why didn't the caller ask for the sculpture?"

Philip shrugged. "I don't know. But right now, all I care about is finding Victoria. I need to know she's safe. And alive." He turned to me. "I need you to find her. I love her more than anything. More than anything in the world."

"So there's a good chance it's someone who's after this sculpture that has her? And blew up your boat?"

"Maybe. But there are a lot of people out there who'd do anything to get this piece—it's a crystal pelican—at any cost."

"It's a pelican?"

Philip nodded. "Almost four feet high. All crystal...almost unheard of at that size."

I watched him, both of us quiet for a moment. "Philip, would you be opposed to me sharing any of what you're telling me with someone from the sheriff's office?"

"No! Do not do that, Henry." He shook his head and again said, "No, you can't do that."

He turned into the Yulee ballfield parking lot. It was dark and most of the crowd had already thinned. Those who remained made their way toward the exit.

"Better get your car before they lock the gate," he said.

"Where will you be?"

GREGORY PAYETTE

"Sit tight. I'll call you. All I ask is you do whatever you can to find Victoria."

He stopped the green Impala behind my Lexus.

"New car?" he said.

I nodded as I opened the passenger door and put my foot on the ground. "I need more information, Philip, if we're going to find Victoria."

"Why not start with Frank? Although you didn't even finish telling me what happened."

I stepped out of the car and leaned inside before I closed the door. "After we went for a ride, I dropped him off."

Chapter 9

BILLY WAS BEHIND THE bar getting ready to open when I went downstairs for a coffee. I told him about meeting Philip, and that I still didn't have much in the way of suspects outside of his crazy brother Frank.

"Why wouldn't Philip just give you names of anyone who might want to hurt him?" He placed a plastic dishwasher rack full of glasses on top of the bar and slid the glasses onto the rack above his head. "Wouldn't surprise me if the list is longer than he'd let on."

I looked up at Billy. I knew he had more to say. And I was right.

"I'm sorry," he said. "I don't know him. But I think I've told you before, there's something about him that rubs me the wrong way."

I shrugged as I sipped my coffee. "Maybe because he's rich, and wants everyone to know?"

Billy laughed. "I get the feeling he'll run over anyone he has to, just to increase his personal wealth. But at some point, it catches up to you..."

"What about you? You're what I'd consider wealthy. But you're not like that."

Billy shrugged. "I have money. Not money like Philip. He looks like he wipes his ass with Benjamins."

"I'll admit, when he first told me he wanted to stay on the boat—and that I'd have to leave—I wanted to throw him right off the dock." I shrugged. "But he's not as bad as he seems, once you get to know him."

Billy looked up toward the front entrance. A small crowd stood outside and looked through the windows. He looked at his watch, "Time to open." He walked around the bar and opened the front door.

One of Billy's regulars, an older gentleman named Earl, used to come in every day with a friend. The two of them would sit there all day and drink. But then the friend died. Earl continued going in, and would show up as soon as Billy'd open the doors. Earl would put back a few gin and tonics, then head to his part-time job pushing carts at a grocery store.

Earl walked past me to his seat at the other end of the bar. "Hey Henry. Was that you I saw on the news?" He sat down on the stool. "Was that the same boat you were living on?"

I nodded.

"I'm sure not everybody likes you—I think you're a decent guy—but hopefully that explosion wasn't meant for you." He smiled and raised the gin and tonic Billy had ready for him before he even sat down.

I looked at my watch and turned toward the door, looking for Alex.

Earl had his head down looking at the newspaper he brought in with him. He held up a page toward me. "Is this your friend?" He pulled the paper back and read from it. "It says, Philip Wetzel, CEO of Wetzel Gem and Jewel, presumed dead in a boating explosion." He looked my way. "He the one who kicked you off your boat?"

"It was actually his boat," I said. "He didn't exactly kick me off, he just—" I got up and walked toward Earl and reached for the paper in front of him. A picture of Philip was printed on the page Earl had opened. "Fourth generation jewelry and gem dealer and CEO of Wetzel Gem and Jewel perishes in boat explosion still under investigation."

Earl held his glass up near his mouth, turned to me and said, "You don't look much like someone who lost a friend."

I gave Earl a straight-lipped smile and nodded. I slid the paper back in front of him, and walked back to my seat on the other end of the bar.

I could feel Billy watching me as I sat down on the stool. He walked toward me, looked down toward Earl then leaned in close over the bar. He kept his voice quiet. "You should brush up on your acting if you want people to believe your friend's really dead."

I looked back at Billy and sipped my coffee, then felt a hand rest on my back. I turned to look over my shoulder.

It was Alex.

Earl stared down from the other end. "Hey, beautiful." He raised his glass to her.

She smiled. "Are you doing all right today, Earl?"

He sipped his drink then raised it again, gave her the same answer he gave everyone. "Still on the right side of the ground."

Alex sat down next to me. "Everything all right?" She looked back and forth from me to Billy. "You both have those looks on your faces..."

I'd already told her what I knew about Philip. So she knew he was alive. She leaned in toward me, looked around and said, "Mike said they're close to considering Philip as presumed dead."

I shrugged. "Nothing I can do about that right now. Not without putting him in danger." I pulled out my phone and looked at the screen. "I'm actually waiting for his call."

From down the other end of the bar, Earl said, "Says here your friend Philip had a falling out with his brother, Frank. Kicked out of the business after the father died." Earl looked my way. "You know the brother?"

"I've met him once or twice." I finished the rest of my coffee and slid my cup forward. "Billy, you mind if Alex and I go upstairs?"

Billy shook his head. "You don't have to ask. I'll move the rest of my stuff out of there later today or tomorrow. It's yours...your official office."

"And bedroom," Alex said with a smile.

"Okay, I just want to be sure you're—"

"Henry, stop talking before I change my mind and lease the space out to someone else...for three times as much." He took my empty cup off the bar. "Aren't you going to eat?"

I got up from my seat and turned to him. "What are you, my mother?"

· · · · ● · ● · · ·

50

I sat at the desk with the computer screen in front of me. "I've been trying to figure out what Frank Wetzel has been up to. It's like he dropped off the face of the earth once he left the business."

Alex sat in the chair next to me. "Did you know he wasn't involved anymore?"

"In the business?" I shook my head. "Had no idea. I didn't talk much with Philip over the last few years. And even before that, it's not like we ever talked business. Really, the most he ever said to me was when I stayed at his house in Ocracoke."

Alex reached down into her backpack and pulled out her laptop. "So he wants you to find Victoria, but he didn't give you a single lead?"

"Besides finding Frank, I'm not sure where to begin. Although, he mentioned a crystal pelican—a sculpture."

"What about it?"

"He wondered if this all had something to do with it. It's a pelican, about three or so feet tall...made of some rare crystal."

"I didn't know you could have a piece of crystal that size."

I shrugged. "I have no idea, to be honest. I don't know if it has to do with any of this or not."

Alex said, "Did he say anything else about that morning at the boat? I mean, you think he was hiding something from you?"

"All I know is he left for a run, bumped into me at the marina, then got the call from Victoria."

Alex looked at the screen on her laptop. "What about—what are their names—Ronnie and Margaret? You said they're normally up early"

"Margaret was out early, said it was a typical morning. Quiet. She did see Philip running, but didn't pay him much attention. It must've been around the same time I ran into him."

"Anyone else around the marina we should talk to?"

"The place has been swarming with cops. Fire and Rescue's Marine division was trolling the water. We should wait for them to clear out. Last thing I need is Stone giving me trouble for asking questions."

"What if we go now? Just say we're getting lunch."

I looked at my watch. "I want to drive out to Darcy Car Rental."

"And what about Frank? If he's out there..."

Alex moved to the window and looked out over the parking lot toward the St. Johns. She turned and said, "You know what happened with Philip and his brother?"

I shook my head. "No. He was actually surprised to hear Frank's around. One thing I can say, Frank didn't look too good."

I turned toward the computer screen and scrolled through the news feed. "Alex, look at this."

Alex looked over my shoulder at the screen.

I pointed to the article:

Wetzel Gem and Jewelry loses millions after rare crystal theft. Believed to be an Inside job.

"When was that?"

"A few years ago. No charges were ever filed."

Alex reached into her backpack and pulled out her laptop. She sat down in a chair against the wall and started reading her screen. "Nobody was ever caught," she said. "Says here, when a reporter called Frank at the office to ask questions, she was told he was no longer with the company."

Chapter 10

Darcy Car Rental was Northside of Jacksonville and not nearly as close to the airport as the bigger national rental agencies. I wondered where they got their business, especially being located deep in the back of an old, outdated industrial park with nothing more than a sign at the entrance listing each business in the park.

On the far end of the long brick building, and to the right of Woody's Custom Cabinets, was Darcy Car Rental. I looked inside the window, but it was hard to see through the glass with tinted film over the windows.

I pulled on the door, but it was locked. The sign read open but that didn't seem to be the case. I looked at my watch. It was eleven-twenty. Too early for them to close for lunch, I thought. I put my face against the glass and used my hands to block the glare from the sun. But I didn't see anybody inside.

I walked around toward the back of the building to see if there was another way in. There was a garage door and it was wide open. But I didn't see anybody back there.

Not at first.

I turned the corner and walked through the open garage doorway. There was a young woman on the concrete floor, face down toward the concrete and her body was soaked in a puddle with water running from the hose.

The hose was wrapped tight around her neck, the pressure from the water built-up inside. The expanding force of the water had created a hard, tight noose.

I followed the end of the hose to the spicket on the wall, turned it off, and hurried back over to the woman and kneeled down beside her. I turned her over, her face pale blue in color. She appeared to be staring back at me, but had no pulse. Her skin was wet but also as cold as the concrete where she lay, dead.

I yelled out for help, feeling around my pockets for my phone but realized I didn't have it with me. Nobody responded to my call for help. There was clearly nobody else in the building. At least not inside Darcy Car Rental.

I ran through a doorway toward the front of the building looking for a phone. Behind the counter, in the customer service area, was a filing cabinet tipped over on its side. I stepped across the floor, covered in papers that had been dumped from the cabinet. I looked for a phone, but there wasn't one. Not that I could see.

One of the papers on the ground caught my eye. I picked it up, saw it was an invoice and noticed a handwritten name across the top. I picked up another...same thing. A handwritten name across the top of the invoice.

There was a computer monitor with wires that dangled over the edge of the counter but no computer. It looked as if it had been taken.

As I ran back toward the back of the building I bent down and grabbed as many of the invoices as I could, then ran through the doorway again, past the poor young woman's body and out through the open garage doorway. I looked back at her body, felt a sense of guilt leaving her there, but there was little I could do.

In the back I ran through a door with a sign above that said, *Woody's Cabinet Shop, please use the front entrance.* I pulled on the door and stepped inside.

My heart raced and my breaths were short.

An older gentleman with a long beard leaned over a table saw. He must not have heard me at first, his head down as he ran a piece of wood through the saw's blade. He turned off the power and lifted the goggles from his eyes. With a nod, he said, "Can I help you?"

"Call nine-one-one," I said. "There's a girl next door...she's dead. Right inside the garage door."

His eyes widened. "At Darcy's?"

"Yes, please! Call nine-one-one!"

The man looked at the pile of papers I held in my hands, placed his goggles down on the saw and ran through another doorway.

I didn't wait, but turned and ran out the back of his shop, past the garage door behind Darcy Car Rental.

I jumped in my car and took off. I drove as fast as I could to get out of there, knowing I couldn't afford to let anyone—especially Mike Stone or anybody else from the JSO—try to pull me into the death of this poor girl.

• • • ● ●● ● • •

Alex was at a desk upstairs in my office above Billy's Place when I arrived.

I threw the invoices down in front of her. "These were all over the floor out front, behind the counter at Darcy Car Rental."

She took one from the top of the pile. "Are we supposed to go through every one of these, try to match the SUV you saw?"

I nodded and took half the pile, sat down on the couch. "We'll split it up. The license plate is written on top. We'll eliminate the ones that don't match." I started going through the pile in my lap. "The thing is, whoever was in there might've already taken the invoice we'd need. And that's assuming what happened at Darcy Rental is even related."

"It might not be," Alex said. "But why didn't you just call Mike? Or wait for someone from the sheriff's office to show up?"

"Because if this does have anything to do with Philip's boat or the SUV I saw at the marina, then I think I'm better off keeping my hands clean. I don't need Mike coming after me, questioning me again for something I had nothing to do with just because I was in the wrong place at the wrong time."

"Why would he come after you?"

"Why wouldn't he? I was there alone."

"You don't even think you should tell him you're the one who saw the poor girl?"

I shook my head. "What good would it do?"

"But you didn't do anything, so I don't understand why..."

I stared back at Alex. "Just trust me for now. I need to stay low. Frank knows I might know where Philip is. And I'm sure he's not the only one. Throw if the sheriff's office starts tailing me... It won't make our job any easier. Especially if I lead someone right to Philip."

We both stayed quiet as we each flipped through the invoices. I knew we weren't in agreement with how much I should tell Mike. But I was right.

Alex held up one of the invoices. "Look at this."

I jumped from the couch as she turned in her seat and held it out to me. "C. Weiss?"

"That's it? No first name?"

She shook her head. "They rented it the day before the explosion. Returned it late the next day."

Alex turned to the computer and I stood over her shoulder as she typed "C. Weiss" into the computer. She turned and looked up at me. "No more than a handful of people with that last name down here. But nobody with a first name starts with a C."

Chapter 11

I SAT OUTSIDE THE Ocean Oaks condominium complex in Neptune Beach. There were five units in total, and I had no idea if Carla Weiss was the C. Weiss we were looking for.

As it turned out, Alex found her name in an old white pages she had laying around her house. I had no idea if Carla Weiss had any connection at all to Philip Wetzel or Darcy Car Rental. But it was worth a shot.

The buildings were older with stained white stucco siding. There wasn't much in the way of landscaping aside from a few flowers planted along the front. For a place called Ocean Oaks, there were only two oaks that I noticed. I guessed they'd been cut down for the retail development across the way.

I looked at the address Alex had given me and walked up three flights of stairs of the garden-style apartment building. A UPS package sat on the ground outside the door of her unit, number three-oh-four. I moved it to the side with my foot and looked down at the name on the label. It was addressed to Carla Weiss.

I knocked on the door. Jimmy Cliff played loud from the other side as I glanced at the peep hole and wondered if anyone was watching me from the other side.

Nobody came to the door, so I knocked again. I used the steel door knocker, and the music was turned down.

I knocked again. "Hello? Anybody home?"

There was a click. A deadbolt popped and slid. The door opened, but only as far as the chain across the top would let it.

Soft, brown eyes looked out from behind the chain holding the door closed. The door was only open five or six inches, but enough for me to see she was dressed in a bikini with a kimono robe.

She stared at me. "Yes?" is all she said with her somewhat raspy voice.

I watched her, no more than a foot away from where she stood. "Are you Carla Weiss?"

She paused, then turned and looked behind her before she answered, "Who are you?"

"Henry Walsh." I gave her a tight-lipped smile. "Are you Miss Carla Weiss?"

She still didn't answer.

"Would you mind if I came inside?" I said.

She stared back at me for a moment. "My boyfriend's sleeping. And I have no idea who you are." She raised an eyebrow and looked me up and down. "Mr. Henry Walsh, I'm sorry but I don't let strangers just walk in my place."

"He can sleep right through Jimmy Cliff like that, huh? Must be a heavy sleeper." I looked past her into the apartment. "Lucky."

Her big brown eyes still watching me, she gave me a nod with her chin. "Why don't you tell me why you're here?" She turned and looked behind her. "You a cop?"

I shook my head and slid her my business card through the opening. She grabbed it with her long fingers. "Walsh Investigations? You're a private investigator?"

"I'd like to ask you a few questions, assuming you are Carla Weiss." I bent down and picked up the small box from the floor. I turned the label toward her. "This for you?"

She closed the door, slid the chain, and opened it again. She pushed the door open and walked away without a word.

I know the smell of pot pretty well and knew the odor floating in the air was just that. And it only intensified as I took a few more steps inside.

There was a square table pushed up against one side of the kitchen with only two chairs on either end of it. There was barely enough room for it, the small amount of space shared by a white refrigerator that seemed to make a lot of noise. The front of it was covered in magnets and pictures. A wooden rack next to the sink was full of dishes and took up half the space on the counter.

Carla—even though she'd yet to confirm at that point that was her name—walked into the adjacent room with a couch, a coffee table, and a small TV that sat on a metal stand across from the couch.

Straight ahead past the furniture was a sliding glass door that led to a balcony. The place wasn't what I'd call high-end, by any means, but the view was worth a million. Nothing but a row of palm trees separated her condo from Neptune Beach.

There were a few plants and an ashtray on the four-foot wall dividing the kitchen from the room with the TV. Inside the ashtray was half a smoked joint. I could smell it in the air.

Carla walked toward the sliding glass door, the end of her kimono robe trailing behind her long, bare legs. She pulled on the handle and opened the door and looked back toward me over her shoulder. "It's for medicinal purposes."

I shrugged. "Not a problem. I hope it's working for you."

She said, "I don't normally let strangers in my home. But you look a little normal." She raised an eyebrow. "Not that I haven't been steered wrong judging a man by his looks."

She walked toward me, reached down and picked up a black, leather purse. She put it over her shoulder and crossed her arms as she stared back at me.

I nodded toward the 9mm in her purse. "You're not going to need that right now."

"So are you going to tell me why you're here? I let a stranger in my place, I'd at least hope he'd have a little more to say."

"The name C. Weiss was found on a document that's of, uh...it's of interest to me. I'm trying to find this person." I looked past her toward the sliding glass door. "You're the only person in the area with that last name and whose first initial is a C."

She watched me for a moment, turned and took a seat on her couch. She placed her purse beside her and turned toward me. "Okay, well I guess you won't be fooled if I told you my name wasn't Carla?"

I stared back at her but didn't even respond.

Carla said, "But you'd have to tell me what this document might be. I have no idea what you're—"

"Have you ever rented a car from Darcy Car Rental?"

She leaned against the back of the couch and pulled a pack of cigarettes from her purse. She took one out, stuck it in her mouth and lit it. She closed her eyes as she took a deep drag. She had one arm folded across the front of her chest, the other up in the air with her two long fingers holding the cigarette up near her mouth. She took another drag, lifted her chin and blew the smoke toward the ceiling. "I've never heard of anyone named Darcy?"

"Darcy Car Rental. Your name—or someone with your last name and same first initial—was on an invoice for a car that was rented from there."

She shrugged her shoulders. "Why would I need to rent a car?"

"I don't know if you're playing games with me, Carla. But if you're going to deny it was you—and I'm not promising I'll believe you—then maybe you know someone else in the area who'd fit the bill?"

She stared up at me for a moment, leaned forward and crushed her cigarette out in the ashtray. She stood up from the couch, made her way out toward the balcony. and turned her head toward me. She gestured for me to follow.

I stepped outside behind her and pulled the door closed behind me.

Carla leaned over the railing, her back to me. Her robe and long blonde hair blew in the gentle, hot breeze. She turned toward me and pulled her kimono closed in front of her. "I'm sorry. I can't help you."

"Are you sure about that? Because, I'll be honest. The way you're acting I'm not sure I'm buying any of this."

She squinted and gave me half a smile. "I don't know what to tell you. Other than it was nice having you." She held out my card. "Okay if I hold onto this?"

I pulled open the screen door, stepped back inside and looked toward her through the doorway. "I'll let myself out. Oh and tell your boyfriend I'm sorry if I woke him up."

She smiled. "If you must know, that is the one thing I lied about. I don't have a boyfriend."

Chapter 12

I LEFT CARLA'S APARTMENT thirsty and hungry. Maybe the secondary smoke from the pot floating in her condo had gotten to me.

I parked on First Street, just after I'd passed a place called Skip's Bar with a bright neon sign just above the faded green awning.

I walked inside and was hit with the smokey essence of a local place. I had the feeling everyone knew I wasn't a regular, the way they all looked at me. I made my way up to the bar where a sign on the wall said, *Established 1939.*

The worn, wooden bar top and a thick cloud of smoke suspended above the crowd gave the place a certain feel you wouldn't find in most places.

The crowd was mixed in both age and attire.

I sat at the bar in the only open seat available. The bartender had a Jack Daniels in my hand before I even had a chance to say hello.

"First time here?" he said.

I looked around the place. "I think I've been here once or twice. Those days are a little foggy."

"That's why people come here." He gave me a smile and a nod and ran a rag along the bar next to me. "Are you on vacation?"

I shook my head. "I wish."

He nodded, as if he understood. "You from around here?"

About to sip my drink, I stopped with my glass in front of my lips. "I live on a boat in a marina on the St. Johns." I took a sip of Jack. "I should say... I used to live on a boat."

He glanced along the bar as he studied each glass in front of his patrons. He walked off and grabbed any empty one and filled it without having to ask what it was.

"What's your name?" I said as he walked past me.

"Jackson."

I raised my glass to him. "Henry."

Jackson reached under the bar and came out with a pack of Marlboros. He stuck a cigarette in his mouth and lit it as he walked to the other end of the long bar. I watched him take a few quick drags, blow the smoke out his nose. He seemed like he just needed to hurry, get as much nicotine into his body as he could in a somewhat condensed smoke break. He put the cigarette in the ashtray then disappeared through a swinging door.

He walked back out within less than a minute, carrying cases of beer. He placed them down on the floor and filled the cooler behind the bar in front of me. He looked up at me. "Ready for another Jack?"

I pushed my empty glass toward him with a nod.

He reached for the bottle and gave me a healthy pour. "So you said you used to live on the St. Johns, huh? Where are you now?"

"Good question," I said as I reached for my drink. "You happen to hear about that boat that exploded over at Trout River Marina?"

He nodded. "Of course."

I took a drink and watched him over the rim of the glass. "That was my boat. Although, not technically. A friend of mine owned it. But that's where I used to live."

Jackson looked past me. "Someone was just in here talking about that. I don't remember who, but..." He paused for a moment. "The guy that was killed...He was a friend of yours?"

"You could say that."

"He'd been in here before, you know. I recognized him when they showed his picture on the TV. Owned a jewelry company or something like that, right?"

I nodded and sipped my Jack.

Jackson walked away and grabbed his burning cigarette from the ashtray at the other end of the bar. He took a drag of what was left and smashed it out.

Three women in bikini tops laughed from about six stools down from me. He went over, asked what they wanted, then reached under the bar and put three cans of Pabst Blue Ribbon in front of them.

I looked at the chalkboard on the wall across from them. Someone had scribbled, *Pabst Blue Ribbon cans two dollars.*

Jackson walked back over and squinted when he looked at me. "The guy'd been in here at one time with a couple who used to come in here all the time together. The wife was older, but real good looking. Her husband—or ex-husband, from what I hear—was a short, chubby guy. Older than her, from what I could tell."

"And they were with Philip Wetzel? You sure?"

He said, "You got a picture of him?"

I pulled out my phone and flicked my finger on the screen. I turned the only picture I had of Philip toward Jackson.

He nodded. "Yeah, that's him. In fact he's been in here more than once."

"You know their names? The couple he was with?"

"The ex-husband's name was Charles. I called him Charlie once. He told me to call him 'Charles.' "

"And the wife?"

Jackson shook his head, looked down toward the ground. "I don't know her name. Like I said, real pretty. There was something about her."

· · · ● ● · ● ● · · ·

After a couple of hours and three-or-four-too-many whiskies I left Skip's. I went looking for a better place to eat, because pickled eggs and Slim Jims weren't going to cut it.

The streets outside were busy for a weeknight and, like Skip's, filled with a mixed crowd enjoying the hot, humid Florida evening.

I didn't know the area well, so I turned down a random side street and followed it for a few blocks. But soon I realized I'd walked away from the crowd and, by the looks of it, any chance of finding a decent place to eat.

The street I was on was mostly residential, with small houses and apartments close to the street. As soon as I turned to walk back in the other direction, I saw a car driving slowly toward me with the headlights on. I stopped and watched it go past me and tried to look inside. But the windows were tinted dark.

I continued to walk away from the car and headed in the opposite direction.

I heard a squeal and turned as the car's reverse lights lit up. The car backed down a side street, turned and again drove toward me.

I continued walking until I heard car doors open and close. I turned and looked behind me. Three men—each wearing sunglasses even though the sun was going down—were coming toward me.

I picked up the pace, but didn't run. I reached in my pocket for my phone and, at that point, wished I'd taken both Alex and Billy's advice to carry a firearm.

One of the men yelled, "Excuse me, sir."

I ignored him and kept moving.

"Hey," he said. "I'm talking to you, buddy. Hold it right there."

I glanced over my shoulder. All three men were stocky. Maybe on the heavy side. I was sure I could outrun all three of them.

So that's what I started to do.

As I ran I heard behind one of the men yell, "Get the car!"

Two of the men continued to follow me on foot but I glanced over my shoulder and realized the distance between us was widening.

I ran as fast as I could and regretted the last two or maybe three shots of Jack I had at Skips. I looked at the North Street sign and hit the next intersection, running in front of the oncoming cars with horns blowing.

I made it across to the other side, but no matter how fast I tried to move, the two men somehow kept up.

I turned down First Street. The crowd was thick and allowed me to blend in while I caught my breath. I didn't turn to look, instead I kept my head down and moving without trying to draw attention.

I spotted a restaurant called Doro and pulled on the front door. But it was locked. The place was closed. As I turned from the door the two men were no more than twenty feet away, moving toward me. One of them had his hand inside his suit coat. The black car they were in—a Cadillac, now that I could see it up close—pulled up along the street. The driver blew the horn. The crowd cleared out of his way.

I stood in front of the restaurant's glass doors. I had nowhere to run. The man's hand was still inside his coat.

He walked straight toward me and pressed a gun into my stomach with his back to the crowd. He grabbed me by the arm and pulled me toward the car parked on the street in front of us. "Get in the car," he said. I felt the heat of his breath on the side of my head. He looked up and down the sidewalk while the other man—my size but thicker with muscle he clearly worked hard for—opened the back passenger door of the car.

I drove my elbow up into the face of the man with the gun, then drove my shoulder into his chest as he caved over. I threw all I had into a punch that sent him stumbling backwards and into the crowd. I ran past the restaurant along the sidewalk and turned hard around the corner of the building onto a dirt path surrounded by trees and overgrown grass.

There was a pop. The people screamed. I had no doubt what it was, and soon felt a burning ache move through my leg. A spot of blood soaked through my jeans.

I heard one of the men yell something but didn't wait to find out what it was, his voice covered in screams from the scurrying crowd.

I dropped down to the ground but pushed myself back up. I ran as best I could with the pain now moving through my body. I knew I'd been shot, and looked over my shoulder as I ran along the side of the building. I expected to see the men but there was nobody behind me.

The black Cadillac roared along North Street, tires squealing, as it turned and disappeared around the corner.

I stopped, holding my thigh with both hands. The spot of blood grew as it soaked further through my pants. I leaned against the brick exterior of the building and slid down to the ground.

Chapter 13

CRUISERS FROM THE NEPTUNE Beach Police Department drove past me at high speeds, sirens blaring. I walked along First Street, trying to hide my limp and blend in with the crowd. I needed to get to my car, which was more than just a few blocks away. I did what I could to ignore the pain.

A group of young men—boys, maybe teenagers—pointed to my leg as they walked by me on the sidewalk. One of the boys said, "You all right, man?" as he looked down at my blood-soaked pants.

I waved my hand and walked past them. "Never been better." I kept moving as best I could, knowing the cops were surely out looking for a man who'd been shot. That was me. I looked down toward the concrete and saw spots of blood next to my foot with each step I took.

I continued north on First, looked up and saw the faded green awning outside Skip's Bar. I limped around the corner, stopped and leaned on the building for a moment. I looked up along the street and spotted my car just a few feet away.

I opened the door and hopped inside, closed the door and slouched down. With my head resting against the back of my seat, I closed my eyes.

The pain in my leg burned. I didn't know for sure but had a feeling the bullet merely grazed my thigh. Maybe it was just wishful thinking at the time, but I hoped there wasn't a bullet inside my leg.

I turned the ignition, looked over my shoulder and pulled out of the space as I reached for my phone to call Alex.

She answered on the first ring. "Henry? Where have you been?"

I winced in pain when I moved my foot from the gas pedal to the brake. "Dodging bullets."

"What?"

"Can you meet me at Billy's?"

"I'm right around the corner, already on my way," she said. "Will you please tell me you're all right?"

There was rarely any fooling Alex. She had innate power, where she'd know before anyone else if someone was skating around the truth.

I said, "I'm ten, fifteen minutes away. We'll talk then." I hung up and leaned forward in my seat as I grabbed the top of the steering with both hands, pulling myself forward trying to relieve the pressure from my thigh.

· · • • • • • · ·

I pulled around back of Billy's parking lot and squeezed between two cars in a tight space so I could park as close to the rear door as possible. I'd lost a fair amount of blood, hadn't eaten all day, and put back more than a handful of drinks.

All I wanted to do was sleep.

I snuck through the back door, cut through the kitchen and hopped my way up the stairs to not only my temporary housing but my place of business for Walsh Investigations.

I hopped across the room, fell back onto the couch, and pulled my blood-soaked pants down past my knees. I was light-headed and leaned my head against the back of the couch and closed my eyes.

I looked up when I heard the door swing open.

Alex rushed to my side without saying a word. She leaned over in front of me, holding my leg. She breathed heavily, nearly out of breath and kneeled down on the floor in front of me. She took off my shoes, then pulled my pants down the rest of the way.

I opened one eye and looked down at the top of her head. "Now's not a good time for that," I said. "I've been shot, you know." I tried to force a smile.

She looked up at me from the tops of her eyes. "Looks like it stopped bleeding." She looked around the room. "Does he have any medical supplies up here?" She got up and walked toward the small bathroom. I heard drawers opening and closing.

"In the closet, behind the door."

A moment later Alex came out with an armful of bandages, an industrial-sized box of band-aids, a bottle of rubbing alcohol, and a white towel.

"I know you don't mind me like this, but can you grab a pair of shorts from my bag?" I nodded toward my duffle bag, tucked under a desk across the room.

She ignored my request for shorts, kneeled down in front of me and poured rubbing alcohol into a gauze pad. She used it to wipe around my wound.

"Jesus, that hurts!" I said. "Be careful."

She looked up at me but continued cleaning the blood from my leg. "Doesn't look that bad," she said.

"No? A lot of blood..."

She got up on the couch and sat next to me. "Let me go see what else Billy has. We need something to seal it up."

"I thought you said it was nothing?"

"I didn't say '*nothing*.' I just said it doesn't look bad. Doesn't mean you don't have a hole in your leg." She got up on her feet and walked toward the stairs. "Be right back."

Alex came out a moment later holding a red, plastic box by the handle and kneeled down next to me. She opened the box and pulled out a roll of tape.

Billy came up the stairs behind her and stood looking down at me over Alex's shoulder. "Jesus," he said. "What the hell'd you do?"

I gave him a look. "Cut myself shaving."

Billy's gaze moved to my blood-soaked pants on the floor. "That's a lot of blood."

"Looks worse than it is," I said.

Alex turned and said to him over her shoulder. "He was shot. Looks like it just got him." She smirked and gave Billy a nod. "Affecting his brain a bit."

"I need to eat," I said. The sting from the rubbing alcohol Alex poured directly onto my thigh made me jump to my feet from the couch. "Take it easy, will you?"

Billy reached for my arm, making sure I was steady on my feet. "Where'd it happen?"

"Neptune Beach. Ever hear of Skip's Bar? Had a few, went out looking for a better place to eat—"

"They have food there, don't they?"

I gave him a look. "Ham sandwiches and Slim Jims." I leaned back down onto the couch. "So I went for a walk, took the wrong turn down a side street. A car drove toward me and next thing I know I'm on the run, trying to get away."

Alex said, "You get a good look at them?"

I shrugged. "To be honest, it's all a little blurry right now."

"From being at Skip's?" Billy said, cracking half a smile.

I watched Alex as she cleaned my leg and rolled tape around my thigh. "That didn't help." I looked up at Billy. "They caught up to me, stuck a gun in my ribs and tried to get me in the car. So I cracked the guy in the face with my elbow. Other one pulled his gun...son of a bitch shot at me as I turned to run...right there in front of the crowd."

Billy, slowly shaking his head. "Nobody called the cops?"

"Everyone ran as soon as he got a shot off. I ran along the side of the building, heard the sirens and just kept going until I got to my car."

Alex kneeled in front of me. "I'll tell you what, that bullet goes two inches the other way and..."

"I know, you don't have to say it. A little close, but I'm trying not to think about what that would've been like."

We were all quiet for a moment, Billy wheeled the wooden chair from my desk and rolled it up next to Alex. He said, "You think this has something to do with Philip?"

I nodded and looked back and forth from Alex to Billy.

Alex stood up in front of me. "I should've gone with you," I said, "Why, so we both get shot?"

Billy said, "Why weren't you armed?"

I pushed myself up from the couch without answering and tried to put a little weight on my leg. "Not bad," I said. Although the truth was, it hurt like hell. I put my hand on Alex's shoulder. "Good work, doc."

"You need to see a *real* doctor," she said.

I shrugged. "Who needs a real one?" I walked with a limp over to the window and looked down toward the parking lot. I hadn't remembered where I parked my car.

Billy walked toward the doorway. "I'll go make you something to eat." He looked around the room. "I know you've been shot, doesn't mean you can't clean up your mess. Blood all over the place...looks like someone got butchered up here."

I turned from the window. "Don't worry, I'll clean it up."

He took a step down the stairs and stopped. "I'm kidding. Come down and have a drink. It heals all wounds."

• • • ● • ● • • •

Billy walked through the swinging door behind the bar from the kitchen, holding a large bowl. He slid it in front of me on the bar. "You'll like this." He gave Alex a nod with his chin. "Jake's putting yours together now."

I turned to Alex. She had a look of concern on her face.

"You all right?" I said.

Her gaze was on me. "I'm worried that... I'm afraid this is more than we can handle. I mean, do you have any idea what Philip's into? You've said it yourself...you're barely friends. If you didn't live on his boat you probably would never talk to him again."

Alex is tough. One of the toughest people I know. At least as far as I could tell, looking from the outside, she was the last person who'd tell someone she was worried. So when her hard shell began to crack, I knew the time had come to listen to what she had to say.

Billy stepped over in front of us on the other side of the bar and nodded toward the bowl. "You try it?"

I picked up the spoon and gave it a taste.

He said. "You like it? It's crab stew. Recipe has been in my family for five generations."

"Five generations? You sure?"

Billy shrugged. "I don't know. Two, three...who knows. Maybe I got it off the internet. Just eat it, will you?"

I sipped the hot stew from my spoon and gave him a nod. "Not bad."

"Not bad? Are you kidding? Best you've ever had, no?"

I gave him a smile and took another sip.

Alex stared across the bar.

I held the end of the spoon toward her. "Want to try it?"

She gave me a look and held it there for a moment. "Are you listening to what I'm saying? You've been shot, Henry. It could've been worse. You could be dead." She put her hand on my arm. "These aren't small-time crooks, Henry."

I put my spoon down on the bar beside my bowl. "I know."

"We don't even know what we're looking for," she said.

I patted the pockets on my pants without answering her. "Shit. Where's my phone?" I pushed my stool out from the bar and leaned on the edge to get myself up on my own two feet.

The pain shot through my leg as I started toward the stairs. "Philip should've called by now. If I missed his call..."

Alex came over to me and grabbed me by the arm. "Sit your ass down." She turned me around and helped me back into the stool, then disappeared up the stairs.

Billy slid two plates down in front of me. One was a sandwich and fries.

I looked at the second plate he'd put down on the bar. "What's that?"

"They're called vegetables," he said. "I promise they won't hurt you."

A few moments later Alex walked up behind me and placed my phone in front of me. "I wiped your blood from the screen."

I pushed the plate of vegetables toward her. "This must be yours." I looked at my phone and saw I had missed calls. A couple from Alex. I said to her, "You called?"

She nodded. "A few times. Told you...I was worried when I didn't hear from you. Guess I had a reason to be."

I had some messages waiting, so I dialed into voicemail. I turned the receiver away from my mouth, as if the voicemail could hear me. I looked around, and in a hushed tone said, "It's Philip." I shook my head. "Shit, I missed his call." I listened, and looked at my watch. "Said he'd call me back at eleven. He wants to meet, but I don't know where or when."

Alex said, "You're in no condition to go anywhere." She looked down at my leg. "You need to see a doctor."

I shook my head. "No, I'm fine. Like I said, you did a fine job." I stirred my soup with my spoon.

Alex picked a carrot from the plate and took a bite. "I'm going with you."

"No, he wants me there alone. And it's probably best for now, anyway."

Alex kept her gaze on me for a moment, shaking her head. "Don't let Philip dictate how this works. He'll only get you in more trouble than you're already in."

Chapter 14

ALEX CONTINUED TO HOUND me in her Jeep, trying to persuade me to go to the ER and have my leg checked-out by—as
she said—a *real* doctor.

"I don't like doctors," I said.

"You don't like doctors?" She smirked. "You're afraid?"

I shook my head. "No. I don't like the whole thing. I don't
like the waiting...sitting in the waiting room. I don't like sitting
in the exam room. Sit and wait, sit and wait."

"That's why you won't go to the doctor? The wait?"

"And I don't trust them. Most of them, anyway. They're
really just people who were good in school. Book smart. Not
much common sense, you ask me. And all the money you have
to pay for, what, two minutes of advice you can get off the
internet?"

She glanced at me. "You're serious."

"All that money you gotta pay. Why, so you can help pay all
that student loan debt?"

Alex rolled her eyes.

"I don't understand people who run to the doctor every time
they have a little scrape or a belly ache."

"You got shot, Henry."

She finally gave up trying to convince me to see a doctor. But she insisted I stay at her house for the night so she could keep an eye on me.

So I agreed.

• • • • ● • ● • • •

Alex held onto my arm and walked me to the spare bedroom on the first floor. It wasn't always the spare bedroom, however. It was originally the bedroom she shared with her husband before he was killed a month after they'd bought the house together.

She looked a bit uneasy standing in the room, looking at the framed photos and paintings on the walls.

I stood in the doorway, just outside the room in the hall. The room was neat and clean and well-decorated. I guess the way a room looked when it didn't get much use. "I can just sleep on the couch," I said. Although I knew the sleep I'd get would beat what I'd gotten on Billy's couch above the restaurant, I felt a little uncomfortable sleeping in this particular bedroom.

But Alex pulled the sheets down. "Are you going to stand out there all night?" She gestured toward the bed. "All yours."

She walked past me and out the door without saying another word. I listened to her footsteps on the hardwoods as she walked down the hall.

She came back a moment later with a glass of water in one hand, a couple of pills in the palm of her other.

I waved my hand back and forth. "I don't need anything," I said. "Pain's not that bad."

She reached for my hand, turned it over, and dropped the pills in my palm. She handed me the glass. "Helps fight infection, which is what you need to worry about right now." She sat down on the edge of the bed.

The only light in the room was the lamp on the table next to me.

"I can't tell you the last time I was in bed this early. At least without passing out."

Her back was to me as she looked down at me over her shoulder and said, "That's why I brought you here. You'd be out there goofing off, as if nothing happened."

I shook my head. "I'd be trying to find whoever shot me. And, of course, looking for Victoria."

She stood up from the bed and looked down at my hand, my palm still facing up, the two pills in my hand. "How long are you going to hold onto that?"

"I'm not one for popping pills," I said.

"You think I'd give you something that wasn't safe?" She reached toward me and pushed up at the bottom of my hand. "It's homeopathic."

"I don't even know what that actually means."

"Just take it, will you? Trust me, for once."

I gave her half a smile and threw the pills into my mouth. I chased them down with the water.

Alex smiled, sat up from the bed and started for the door.

I reached up, grabbed her by the wrist and looked her in the eye. "Hey," I said. "Thank you for taking care of me." I let my hand slide from her wrist but held onto her hand.

She gave my hand a squeeze and smiled without saying a word, leaning over to kiss me on the forehead, like a mother taking care of her little boy.

She turned, flipped off the light, and left the room.

• • • ● • ● • • • ·

It was five in the morning when Philip called and asked me to meet him at Friendship Fountain. When I told him Alex was going to come, he didn't object. So we both got dressed and headed out the door while the sun was still coming up.

The only car we saw when we arrived was Philip's green Impala. I parked next to it and looked in, but he wasn't in the driver's seat.

We stepped from my car and the man with the beard and a baseball cap caught my eye. He had a backpack over his shoulder. I knew it was Philip and walked toward him.

As we approached him, the fountain's water crashed and made it hard to hear what he was saying.

I guess that's exactly why Philip wanted us to meet there.

He looked down at my bare leg. "What happened?"

"Just a scratch," I said. "Philip, you remember Alex?"

He nodded. "How could I forget Alex?" He reached out and shook her hand, shifted his gaze to me and said, "Can I trust her?"

"Alex and I work together," I said. "If you trust me, you can trust her." I looked down at my leg. "And I might need her to protect me."

"Are you going to tell me what happened?"

"I was shot last night. Three men followed me. I was out at Neptune Beach."

"Neptune Beach?"

"At a place called Skip's Bar. I understand you know what I'm talking about."

Philip stared back at me without a response.

"Why don't you tell me about Charles Weiss?" I said.

Philip removed his baseball hat and scratched his head, looking at my leg. "He did that?"

"No. But you know him, right?"

Philip hesitated for a moment. "Yes, I do."

"Then why don't you tell me what the hell's going on? You're leaving me in the dark...sneaking around in your Halloween costume. But I need to know exactly what the hell I'm dealing with here...before one of us really does get killed."

"I ... I don't know what you expect me to tell you, Henry. I was hoping you'd have something to tell me."

I took a deep breath, my hands on my hips. I turned and looked toward the fountain. "I spoke with Carla Weiss."

"Carla?"

"She played dumb with me though. Then come to find out you and Charles and Carla were seen together at Skip's."

Philip removed his sunglasses and narrowed his eyes. "You're right, I haven't told you everything. But you've clearly managed to get some traction on your own." He gave me a quick nod with a forced smile. "That's admirable."

I stared back at him for a moment as I processed his condescending tone. "Philip, the car I saw leaving the marina the morning of the explosion was a rental car. And as far as I could tell, the person who rented it had a last name of Weiss. There was no first name. Only an initial. The letter 'C.' "

"It was Charles? Or Carla?"

"I don't know." I hesitated. "I haven't talked to him. And Carla claims to know nothing about anything. Although I didn't expect much from her."

"So how'd you find out?"

"Find out what?"

"Who rented the car."

I turned, looked at Alex. "We traced the plate, found out it was registered to Darcy Car Rental. I found a poor girl there who'd been strangled to death. Had a hose wrapped around her neck."

Philip closed his eyes, shaking his head. "Charles wouldn't do that. I'm not saying he's a saint. Far from it. But a killer? Not Charles."

Alex and I exchanged a look.

"Here's the thing, Philip. Nothing about this smells right. Your brother puts a gun in my face. I visit the woman with the same last name and initials as her husband, someone who—"

"Ex-husband."

I stared back at Philip, annoyed with his insignificant piece of information. He was feeding me bits of a story but leaving most of it out. "I guess what's concerning me a bit here, Philip, is why you haven't even asked about Victoria. Unless you know something else you're not telling me?"

Philip's head went from a nod to a shake. He seemed unsure how to react. "Christ, Henry. You don't think I want to find her? She means everything to me, and I—"

"You what? Do you know where she is? Or who's responsible?"

"I don't...I mean...is that what you think of me? You think I'm playing some game with you?"

"With me? Not necessarily, but I can't help but wonder if someone really took her?" I stepped closer to him, my arms crossed. I had nothing to go by, my accusation somewhat baseless. But nothing felt right. "I just don't understand," I said. "Why would someone ask for a ransom, then try to kill you? Kind of hard to get money from a dead man."

"I ... I know what it looks like. But I'm not lying about any of this. And Victoria, the love of my life ... I have no idea where she is."

"But you're in trouble. We know that. We know you're hiding from someone. So why don't you tell me who it is? Or who it could be. Help me out."

"I told you what they could be after." Philip put his hands in his pockets, looking toward the ground. He lifted his gaze to mine. "The crystal pelican."

Alex turned around, looking across the park and the area around the fountain. She said to me, "Is it even safe to be standing out here in the open?"

Philip shrugged. "As long as nobody followed you here." He pulled on his fake beard. "Unless you don't think the disguise is good enough?"

"They know I'm involved," I said. "So far, it seems somebody's watching my every move." I looked back at Alex. "You're right. Maybe this isn't safe, to be out in the open like this."

Philip handed me the backpack he had on his shoulder.

"What's this?"

"Fifty grand in cash. You find Victoria, you'll get another fifty."

I held the bag and peaked inside. "A hundred thousand?"

Philip nodded. "Is it not enough?" He turned and sat on a bench on the edge of the stone pathway where we stood. He removed his hat and sunglasses and wiped his brow with his arm.

Alex looked down at Philip. "What are you doing?"

He gazed up at her. "I'm sitting down." He put his hands on his knees and took a deep breath. "Charles Weiss used to be an art collector. He was the best of the best, at one time." Philip looked past me at the fountain. He had a glazed look as he spoke. He squinted. "He used to live in Paris. Those were the days...he made a lot of money. Not just for himself, but for others, too. People like my father."

"Charles knew your father?"

He nodded. "A year or so before he died, they were working on a deal. They had an agreement—a handshake, really—where Charles would help my father invest in the explosion of fine crystal sculptures. Most of them were coming from France and the well-known artists who had all the talent in the world. But they didn't understand the art of the deal."

"Was he a business partner?"

Philip looked at me, but didn't answer. "After my father died, Charles persuaded my brother to work with him on a deal that'd fallen through just before my father's death. You see, he was the money behind the deals. Charles had already had an arrangement with an artist my father adored. I should say, he loved his work. But with my father gone he needed someone in our company who could get the deal back on track."

"Why not you?"

"Charles didn't trust me. And I didn't trust him."

"So Frank partnered with him? Behind your back?"

"I don't know if it was behind my back. But of course—as is always the case with Frank—he bit off more than he could chew. Made big promises he couldn't keep." Philip slid his sunglasses back on his face. "I controlled the money. Without my blessing, Frank couldn't pay Charles for a crystal sculpture that'd already been delivered to my father."

"The pelican?" I said.

Philip nodded.

"But if he'd already delivered it to your father, then why didn't you pay him?"

Philip looked up at me over the top of his glasses. "Like I said, it was a backroom deal with Charles and my father. I didn't know the exact details, other than what Charles had tried to tell me. To me, it was a personal investment. And when my father passed away, as far as I was concerned, their deal was dead. "

I folded my arms at my chest. "So where is it now?"

Philip looked at me but didn't answer. "That doesn't matter. We need to find Victoria...that's all I care about."

Alex said, "Did you say this piece—the sculpture—is a pelican?"

Philip stood from the bench and pulled his hat onto his head. "It's a crystal sculpture." He held his hand off the ground, below his waist. "It's over three-and-a-half feet tall, almost four. An extremely rare sculpture, hand sculpted by the great Francois de Pierre."

"What's the value?"

Philip looked off for a moment. "Two-point-five."

Alex swallowed hard. "Two-point-five *what*?"

Philip looked right at Alex. "Million."

Chapter 15

ALEX AND I WERE back at her house so we could dig a little deeper into not only Charles and Carla Weiss, but Philip's brother Frank.

Alex turned the screen toward me. "This him?"

I nodded. "Yeah, that's Frank. It's an old photo though. He doesn't have that much hair anymore."

"Looks like a rug," she said, staring at the photo on her screen. "Served three years in Calhoun State Prison—"

"Calhoun, in Georgia?"

She nodded. "Failed attempt at robbing a bank. Never made it out the door...security guard heard him talking on his cell phone, said he was about to rob a bank."

"I guess Philip got all the brains in the family," I said.

Alex nodded. "Guard hit him with a stun gun and called the cops. Found with a .22 pistol and a demand note in his pocket." She skimmed through the other search results. "Looks like he moved to France after his sentence. Maybe with Charles Weiss?" She turned and looked at me over her shoulder. "Spent a few weeks in jail over there."

"For what?"

"He robbed someone at gunpoint, at an ATM. The whole thing caught on video." She let out a snort, shaking her head. "What'd Philip say it'd been, a few years since he last saw him?"

"Two or three years."

"You don't believe him?"

I said, "I guess it's true. I don't know Philip very well. Not sure I trust anything coming out of his mouth right now, either. Truth is, if he didn't need someone to watch his boat while he traveled, we wouldn't have had any reason to stay in touch."

Alex got up from the desk and walked into the kitchen.

She came out a moment later and handed me a cup of coffee as she sipped from her own cup...a tea bag string hanging off the side.

Her phone rang. She looked around and shuffled the papers on top of the coffee table. "Where is it?"

The rings continued.

She reached down into the couch cushions, came up with her phone and answered it. "Hello?" She watched me, listening to the call. "That's great, I appreciate it, Claire. I owe you." She was quiet for a moment, grabbed a pad and started writing. "You're right. I will. I'll call you."

Alex tapped her screen and placed the phone on top of the coffee table. She turned the paper out in front of her. "Frank lives in an apartment off of Firestone Road, toward Westside."

"You look excited," I said.

"Excited? How so?"

"Like you love this stuff. You're doing what you're meant to be doing."

She cracked half a smile with a slight shrug of her shoulder.

Alex and I had similar backgrounds. Both in law enforcement with jobs—careers—that didn't quite go as planned. We both tried to make the most of running the security staff for the Jacksonville Sharks baseball team. But getting licensed as a private investigator and going out on my own was what made the most sense to me. It took Alex a little longer and the team being sold to get her to come along with me.

One thing we didn't have in common was a love for guns. Alex grew up with a dad who took her hunting on weekends and holidays, although it didn't take her long to realize shooting an animal wasn't what she'd hoped for.

Her first animal kill was a squirrel, when she was nine.

Turns out, it was also her last.

She admitted she'd have little problem plugging someone if it meant protecting the innocent or someone she cared about. But killing an animal? She never even had a piece of meat again after shooting that squirrel.

Alex got up and walked to her closet door. It had two locks, one on top and one on the bottom. She turned each with a key and pulled the door open, stepped inside and looked toward the back wall and her collection of firearms.

She turned to me and with a nod she said, "About time you carry, at least to protect yourself. Don't you think?"

I didn't answer.

She reached inside, turned and held the handle of a gun toward me.

I grabbed it from her hand.

"My Glock," she said. "It's a 9mm. I want you to hold onto it."

"But I—"

"Henry, you've had a gun pointed at your head. You've been chased and you've been shot. Carrying this won't kill you. But walking around with nothing might."

I held my two bare hands out in front of me, turned them back and forth for Alex. "You say that like these weapons—my bare hands—aren't good enough?" I smiled.

She shook her head, turning to lock the door.

• • • ● • ● • ● • •

I sat shotgun in the passenger seat as we headed south on 295 toward the address Alex's friend from the DMV had given us. It was Frank's last known address on file, and it seemed to be the only one we could find.

Just off the highway and after a couple of quick turns, we pulled into what we hoped was Frank's apartment complex. It was an older, brick building with concrete and steel steps leading up three stories. The wood trim on the windows was a faded gray with peeling paint. There wasn't much color to the place other than potted flowers out on a handful of the concrete patios on the ground floor.

Alex walked ahead of me on our way up the stairs to the third floor. I tried to hide my limp as I followed behind her, but my thigh burned with each step I took.

We stood side-by-side at the door to apartment three-one-oh-two. I checked the folded paper I had in my pocket. "This is the place."

Alex adjusted the holster she wore under her shirt as I knocked on the door. I had the Glock—the one Alex gave me—tucked in the waist of my pants. Both of us were prepared for Frank, who'd already waved his gun around when he first jumped in my car.

I put my ear against the door to listen, but couldn't hear anything inside. I knocked.

Nobody came to the door.

I knocked again. I walked across the decking outside the apartment, leaned on the railing and looked down over the parking lot. I turned to Alex. "Did she tell you what kind of car he drove?"

She shook her head. "Nothing registered under his name," she said. "His license expired."

A woman with two kids in tow and what looked like another one in the oven—at least from where I stood on the third floor—walked across the parking lot from the apartments. She opened the back door of a small blue Toyota Corolla and helped each kid into the back seat. She reached inside the driver's side and the trunk popped open.

Voices came from the stairway, getting louder along with footsteps coming up the stairs.

A male voice said, "Then what about Goodfellas?"

Another man's voice answered, "Nope, doesn't even compare. You're just a racist. Just because the man's black, you think—"

Frank and a younger man, thin and tall with a white tank top and red shorts that went far past his knees, stood in front of me at the top of the stairs. Neither said a word.

Frank was in the middle of eating a burger. His chewing slowed as he stared back at me.

The other one—a kid who looked a lot younger than Frank— was eating fries from a bag that had Burger Brothers printed on the side.

"Good to see you, Frank," I said.

Without saying another word he threw his half-eaten burger at me. Ketchup and mustard exploded on my shirt.

Frank took off down the stairs.

The kid's eyes widened, a fry hanging from his mouth. Before I had a chance to move he turned and ran down the stairs right behind Frank. He dropped his bag...fries went everywhere.

Alex and I ran down the stairs after them, although Frank and the kid had a pretty good lead.

"Frank!" I yelled. "I just want to talk." I looked out toward the parking lot and saw Frank was running fast, moving well between the cars for someone who didn't appear to be in the best physical shape.

I moved like the gimp but ran as fast as I could. The pain in my leg shot through my body. I looked down as blood seeped through the bandage on my leg.

Alex passed me on the stairs and reached for the kid's shirt as he lost his footing and hit the sidewalk after the last step. He tumbled forward and skidded along the ground into a small strip of grass on the edge of the parking lot.

Alex pulled her gun and held it over him. "Stay down," she snapped.

I stopped on the third step, just above Alex and the kid, and looked across the parking lot as Frank grabbed the pregnant woman with the two kids, pulled her from the car and threw her to the ground.

I ran toward them. The women's two kids jumped from the back seat, screaming for their mother, helping her from the ground.

Frank jumped in the front seat, started the car, and took off for the exit. The engine made a whining sound as he gave it more than it could handle, driving full speed across the lot. The tires squealed when Frank took a sharp turn. He jumped the curb and the car bounced from the lot and disappeared onto Firestone Road.

I helped the woman to her feet as she cried and spoke to her children in Spanish. I raised my voice not only because I assumed she didn't speak English but because I thought, for some reason, speaking louder helped the language barrier. "Are you okay?" I said. Her two children cried.

"Yes, I am okay," she said in perfect English. She shook her head. "My car..."

Chapter 16

WE STOOD WITH THE kid by Alex's Jeep, blood dripping from his knees after his fall at the bottom of the stairs.

"Looks like Frank left you high and dry," I said.

He turned over his elbow and looked at the blood dripping down toward his wrist. "You cops?"

Alex and I gave each other a look. I thought maybe we should tell him we were.

"No, we're not cops," Alex said.

I gave him a nod with my chin. "You got a name?"

"I got a name? What kinda question is that?"

With a stare I thought might intimidate him—but didn't—I said, "Can you just tell me your name?"

"If you ain't cops, I don't gotta tell you shit."

Alex waved her 9mm toward him. "This enough for you to talk?"

"What, you gonna shoot me, I don't talk?" He looked down toward the ground. "Name's Jayray."

"Jayray?" I said. "Your middle name's Ray?"

He shook his head. "Unh uh. Jayray. Just like it sounds."

I said, "Is that your apartment up there?"

"No. It's Frank's."

I narrowed my eyes, looking down at the kid. "So why'd you run when you saw us?"

He shrugged. "Frank ran. Figured he knew something...thought you were cops I guess."

"Good guy like that, huh? Takes off on you?" Jayray leaned back against the back of Alex's Jeep, his arms crossed, gazing around the parking lot. "So what do you need me for? I gotta be somewhere."

"I'm looking for someone and I thought Frank might be able to help. Happens to be Frank's brother's fiancé. You know Frank's brother?"

Jayray shook his head.

I wasn't buying it. "No?" I said. "You don't know Philip?"

Jayray kept his arms folded below his chest, the muscles on his boney arms tense.

"We came by to see if Frank knew anything about Philip's fiancé. Also thought I'd see how he made out after he came to see me the other day."

"He know who you are?"

I nodded. "He found me, said he was looking for Philip." I stepped toward him, my face not far from his. "You know nothing about any of this?"

Jayray stepped aside and took a couple of steps away from me. "Why you askin' all these questions like you a cop, but you say you ain't?"

"We're private investigators."

Jayray shrugged. "Same thing, ain'it?" He gave Alex a quick look. "Frank mentioned something about going to see some investigator the other day. Must've been you. Came back all

99

banged up, like it didn't go too well. Said he had to walk ten miles home. But Frank exaggerates a bit. Never know what he's sayin's true or not."

"So what's a kid like you doing, hanging around a guy like Frank? Don't tell me you're just some innocent kid, looking for a father-figure."

Jayray looked past me, again shifting his gaze around the lot.

I gave Alex a nod and she stepped behind him, making sure he didn't try to get too far. She said, "If you'd rather talk to someone from the sheriff's office—answer their questions—I can arrange that. I have good friends over there, you know."

I nodded, looking right at Jayray. "She does know a lot of people there. But I'm thinking you're better off talking to us."

Jayray looked down toward the ground but didn't speak.

I leaned my back against the Jeep. "How old are you?" I said.

"Twenty-three."

I straightened myself up off the back of the Jeep. "Yeah? You don't look a day over seventeen."

"You don't look a day under forty," he said.

"I'll take that as a compliment."

The way Jayray kept looking around the lot, I was sure he was waiting for the right time to make a break.

"So, go ahead and tell me. What is it you do with Frank, just kidnappings? Or are you helping Frank get money from his only brother?"

Jayray stared straight back at me without answering.

I turned to Alex. "Why don't you give Detective Stone a call, see if he'd like a chat with Jayray, maybe he can get him to talk?"

"I didn't do nothin'," Jayray said.

"Go ahead, Alex, give him the detective a call." I pulled out the Glock Alex had given me, held it down by my side. I said to Alex, "I'll make sure Jayray doesn't go anywhere."

Jayray looked down at my gun. "You don't need that thing. I ain't goin' no-where." He put up his hands near his shoulders. "Okay, listen. I don't know the whole story, but I guess Frank's involved in something that has to do with some crystal bird or...something like that."

I turned, Alex and I exchanged looks.

"You know where it is?" I said.

Jayray shook his head. "I don't know much about it at all. Frank doesn't tell me everything."

"Does he know where it is?"

Jayray shook his head. "He's looking for it."

"Did you help Frank kidnap Victoria? Frank hoping his brother'd lead him to the sculpture?"

"No, man, I'm telling you. I got nothing to do with that."

"But you know about the bird."

"I only heard about it. I got nothing to do with it." Jayray looked me straight in the eye without flinching. I didn't want to believe him but something told me he was telling the truth.

"You got a key?" I said.

"Key to what?"

I folded my arms in front of my chest, still holding the Glock in my hand, shaking the muzzle toward Jayray. "Next time you answer another question with a question I'm going to be forced to use this thing." I looked down at the gun in my hand. "And I don't like shooting people. I don't even like guns."

He gave me a cool nod, cracked a piece of a smile. He turned to Alex, gave her the same cool look.

I said, "Come on, Jayray. I'd like to get inside that apartment. You got a key or not?"

Jayray shook his head. "I don't have a key."

I turned to Alex and as soon as I moved my head, Jayray took off like a bullet. He was across the lot and straight out into the street. He ran across oncoming cars and somehow made it to the other side.

He didn't look back.

"Shit," I said.

Alex gave me a look. "I turned my back for one second...you let him get away?"

"What was I supposed to do?" I said. "Shoot him?"

· · · · ● · ● · · ·

We followed the sign toward the office of the apartment complex, around the other side of the building.

We walked in the office and behind a desk was a woman who didn't look like she wanted to be bothered.

"Yes?" she said, barely making any eye contact.

"My name's Henry Walsh. I'm a private investigator investigating a possible kidnapping. And I'm afraid one of your tenants may be involved."

"Got a badge?"

"I'm a private investigator." I pulled out my card and placed it on her desk. She picked it up, took a quick look and handed it back to me.

"You can keep it," I said. "You never know."

She lifted her gaze toward me, her elbow on the desk and her chin in her hand. "Sorry, unless you're with the sheriff's office

I can't let you in. I don't care if you're a private detective or whatever you might be. Can't do it."

I opened my mouth to argue, but Alex grabbed me by the arm. "Come on." She dragged me backwards toward the door, the woman behind the desk already back to what she was doing when we walked in.

We stepped outside.

"She was very pleasant," I said and rolled my eyes. "You know how to pick a lock?"

Alex gave me a look, not saying a word.

"Is that a yes?"

She nodded. "Of course I do."

"What do you mean 'of course you do'?"

"I mean it as I said it. Of course I know how to pick a lock." She walked ahead of me on the stairs and over her shoulder said, "You've never picked a lock?"

I didn't bother answering.

We made it up to the third floor and put her hand out. "Give me a credit card."

I pulled my wallet from my pants, removed a card and placed it in her hand. "You're going to get in with this?"

She didn't answer, her back to me as she slid the card in the crack of the door. "The way they make the lock on these cheap apartments, if they didn't slide the bolt closed we can get it. And if they just went down the street for a burger..." I tried to look over her shoulder, her body pressed tight against the door. Her arms moved up and down from behind, like she was doing surgery or something. She had one hand on the knob, the other moved the card up and down.

"Don't ruin my card," I said. "It's the only one I have."

She ignored me and kept working the lock. Turned and looked at me with a smile and pushed the door open wide.

I stepped sideways and brushed past her to go inside.

A TV was on, but the volume was down. It was set up across from a couch against the opposite wall. The standard apartment set up, I guessed. There was a white pillow that belonged to a bed and a sheet in a ball, pushed to the far side on the couch.

We walked through the room and I opened the first door I saw. It was an empty closet, although it had a horrible smell to it, one that was trapped inside until I let it out.

I closed the door and walked past the TV.

I opened another door that led to a bedroom with a mattress on the floor, pushed up in the far corner. There was a small lamp on the floor next to it and a can of Pabst Blue Ribbon tipped on its side.

Alex walked past me and opened a door from the bedroom. It opened to a bathroom. I peaked inside as she crouched down and opened the doors on a vanity. "It's empty," she said. "Not even a towel or bar of soap."

"What's this guy's deal?" I said. "Lives like a homeless person. But with an apartment."

Chapter 17

ALEX STOOD AGAINST THE wall to the side of the door to Carla's apartment, number three-oh-four. Loud music played on the other side of the door, but went quiet as I was about to knock.

As my knuckles were about to tap the door it opened in front of me.

Carla stood in the doorway with a purse over her shoulder and a tight skirt that stopped halfway down her thighs. I looked past her, the lights in the apartment off but the sunlight kept the place bright.

"Oh, hello. I wasn't expecting anyone to be standing at my door." She squinted. "Harry, right?"

I glanced at Alex with a look on her face like she was trying to hold back a smile.

"Henry." I tilted a nod to my right. "This is Alex."

Carla stepped over the threshold and gave Alex a quick look. The strong smell of weed floated from the inside of her apartment, but almost covered up by the strong, sweet smell of perfume.

"I'm on my way out," she said as she pulled the door closed behind her. She turned and locked the door with her key. "I'm not sure if you're looking for something, but I—"

"Actually, I'd like to know who you told I was here the other day."

She started for the stairs. "I'm sorry, I'm kind of in a hurry."

Alex and I followed behind her.

Her heels clicked on each step. "I didn't tell anyone you were here." She gave me a quick look over her shoulder. "Why?"

"Well, someone came after me. After I'd left."

She got to the bottom of the stairs, turned and looked down at my leg and the blood that had seeped through the bandage after chasing Frank and Jayray. She lifted her sunglasses from her tired, bloodshot eyes. "What happened?"

"Like I said. Someone came after me. And this is why I'd like to know who you told I was here. Because it's from a bullet. You know? From a gun?"

She turned toward the parking lot, up on her toes, scanning the area and looking past the line of tall bushes in front of us, separating the sidewalk from the lot.

A cab pulled up and stopped at the end of the walkway. "I'm sorry about your leg," she said as she walked toward the cab. She didn't look back, ducked inside the cab and took off.

Alex said, "If I had to guess, she knows something."

• • • • • • • • • •

We stopped at Skip's Bar. The crowd was much thinner than it was the day before. Jackson sat at a stool at the far end of the bar drinking from a coffee cup and a cigarette in his hand.

I sat on the stool beside him. "Jackson, remember me?"

He turned and looked at me. The bags under his eyes and unshaved face made him look like he'd aged ten years from when I'd first met him.

"I was here yesterday, asking about Charles Weiss."

"Oh, right. Sorry. A little out of it today." Jackson took a deep drag of his cigarette, drew it all the way down to the filter, then crushed it out in the ashtray. "Henry, right?" He grabbed his cup and stepped around to the other side of the bar.

We ordered drinks, and Jackson put them down on the bar in front of us. He leaned with his hands wide on the bar. "Someone came in asking about you last night."

Alex and I exchanged looks. I said to him, "You know who?"

Jackson shook his head. "Never seen him before. Older gentleman. Wore a suit."

"What'd he say?"

"Asked who you were...what you were asking about."

Alex turned to me for a moment. She looked at Jackson. "What'd you tell them?"

He looked back at her but didn't answer, cocked his head with a crooked smile on his face. "Who's she?"

"Oh, sorry," I said. "Jackson, this is Alex. Alex...Jackson."

He nodded toward her. "Just checkin'."

The door to the place opened behind us with bright sunlight that filled what was mostly a dim place. An old man shuffled his feet past us. I watched as he pulled himself up onto a stool at the far end of the bar from where we sat.

"Hey Enis," Jackson said with a nod. "Be right there." He turned back to me. "Let me take care of my friend. Be right back."

Jackson grabbed a glass, stopped at the beer tab and filled it to the top with a Miller High Life draft. He walked it down to the old man and placed it down on the bar in front of him.

Jackson came back down to our end of the bar. "I didn't tell them anything. Said I didn't know who you are—which is the truth—and you hadn't asked me any questions." He gave me a nod. "Have anything to do with your leg?"

I looked down at my thigh, the bandage red from all the recent action. I nodded. "Some men came after me after I left here. Both on the heavy side. Dressed the way you described. More fat than muscle, from what I could tell."

Jackson nodded. "Sounds like the guy who was in here. Accent like he was from up north. New York, maybe. Real attitude, you know?" He cracked a smile. "I spent a summer bartending up on Cape Cod. Thought it would be like down here, right on the water. Looks nice on paper, you know?" He reached for his coffee cup and took a sip. "People'd come in, I'd tell them I'm from Florida. They'd say people called them *Massholes*, say it like they were proud of it."

"I spent a few years in Rhode Island," I said. "I know what it's like. Massachusetts, Rhode Island, New York...something in the air."

Jackson nodded. "Yeah...cold, shitty weather. That's what it is." He pulled a pack of cigarettes from his shirt pocket, stuck one in his mouth. "What'd you do up in Rhode Island?"

I held my glass up near my mouth. "Was a cop...a detective for a handful of days. Like they say when a ballplayer makes it to the majors, gets sent back down before his pants get dirty...I had a cup of coffee in the big leagues."

Jackson stared back at me. "Never heard that before."

"Didn't last long, that's all."

He lit his cigarette and walked away to the other end of the bar.

I turned toward Alex. "I don't think he said anything to anybody. Someone could've overheard me talking to him, asking questions. Or maybe Carla told someone I was at her place."

Jackson moved up and down the bar, guests starting to pile in. It was right about that time in the day, I guessed. A couple of younger women wearing bikini tops and cut-off jeans came over and sat a few seats down from us. The seats at the bar started to fill.

Alex stared at her phone, then looked up. "Looks like this is him." She showed me the picture.

"Who?"

"Charles Weiss."

I took the phone from her hand. He was an older man, a little heavy but not what I'd call fat. He had white hair and was mostly bald on top. I couldn't picture him with Carla. She wasn't exactly what you'd call a spring chicken, but much younger—and more attractive—than Charles Weiss. "Where'd you get the picture?"

"An event for something called the Jacksonville Gem and Mineral Society."

"The what?"

"Jacksonville Gem and Mineral Society. Looks like jewel collectors...an organization for dealers, I guess." She pulled the phone from my hand and looked back down at the screen.

Chapter 18

THE BUILDING THAT HOUSED the Jacksonville Gem and Mineral Society appeared to be nothing more than a wood-framed barn or an Elk's Club, or a place the angry militia might meet to plan their government takeover.

I pulled on the door, but it was locked. Then reached out and rang the doorbell. I stepped down off the stairs and waited, my eye catching a camera up above my head. I looked up and smiled. "Maybe they're not here," I said.

Then the door opened. An elderly woman stood in the doorway, staring at me and Alex. "Can I help you?" she said. She had a lack of excitement or emotion in her voice. She turned and walked away, leaving the door wide open in front of us.

Alex and I walked in behind her.

The old woman sat down at a round table covered in wood boxes that looked to be filled with jewelry. There were more tables like it, all with a similar box or two on top, with four red plastic chairs around each. It looked like a little kid's classroom. There was even a lectern toward the front of the room with an overhead projector next to it. One wall had a large, green, cloth banner that read Jacksonville Gem and Mineral Society, Established 1959.

The old woman kept her head down as she picked beads out of the wooden boxes and fiddled with them between her fingers. She acted as if she'd forgotten we were there.

Another woman—much younger and taller than the other woman—walked into the room where we were standing and stopped, mid-step. She looked surprised, her gaze toward me. "How'd you get in here?" she said.

"We rang the doorbell." I nodded with my chin toward the old woman. "She let us in."

The younger woman shook her head, her hands on her hips. "I was out back. I'm sorry, but we're not even open right now. We keep these doors locked for a reason, as I'm sure you understand."

I really didn't understand, but assumed she meant there was some value in the jewels or gems or whatever they had in the place.

"Annie?" she said.

The old woman kept her head down, stringing the beads as if she didn't hear her.

"Annie?"

The old woman looked up.

"You have to be careful. Can't just let anybody you want inside."

The old woman smiled, looked up and me and Alex then turned to the younger woman. "They look like a fine young couple, don't they?"

The younger woman turned to us. "I'm Julie Sanders, Executive Director of the Society." She looked down toward the old woman. "This is Annie. She's one of the senior members who comes here to make jewelry. Today wasn't her regular day but she likes to stick around. I don't mind."

The old woman, Annie, glanced up at Alex then went back to what she was doing.

"I'm Henry Walsh. This is Alex Jepson."

Julie smiled, although it seemed quite forced. "So, is there something I can help you with?"

I nodded. "We're looking for someone who may be a member here."

She looked around the empty room. "As you can see, there's nobody else here today. And we don't have another meeting until next month."

I pulled out my phone and turned the screen toward her. "I'm looking for Charles Weiss. Found his picture online, at one of your events."

She took one look and seemed to roll her eyes in disgust. "Mr. Weiss is no longer a member. I'm sorry."

"You sure?" Alex said.

Julie took a hard swallow. "If you're looking for Mr. Weiss, try one of the local bars. As I said, he is no longer a member of the Society."

I pulled out my business card and handed it to her.

She looked down at the card. "Walsh Investigations?" She placed the card down on the table next to her. "What has he done now?"

"To be honest, I can't really say. I don't know if he's done anything at all. But I do need to find him, ask some questions. That's why, when we saw this photo at the event, we thought we'd come by, see if you could help."

"He tried to steal a very valuable piece from one of the other members. He took advantage of the poor man, and has since had his membership revoked. Everybody knew Charles had his eyes on this particular gem stone. And it was no surprise when he tried to take it. Sadly, the only one who didn't know Charles would do such a thing was the poor man he tried to steal it from."

"I don't understand," I said.

"Charles knows gem and mineral values as well as anyone. He has an extensive background working with artists. But when he first offered to run the appraisals table at our event, I was hesitant. He has somewhat of a history I was warned about."

Alex said, "What's the appraisal table?"

"Free appraisals for the attendees to our show." She folded her arms at her chest. "The gentleman, the poor old man with the gem, brought it to the table. Charles appraised it for him—a real lowball number—and then offered to buy it from him right then and there."

"Isn't that how it works?"

She shook her head. "Not at our events. He was there to offer free appraisals, as a gift to attendees. Not to score gems at wholesale costs."

"So how'd you find out?"

"We all knew it was worth something of value. One of our oldest and most knowledgeable members overheard Charles say it was worth two hundred dollars. Then he had the nerve to offer him one-fifty. Cash. She heard him say not to mention it to anyone, he'd pay him after the show."

"What was it, anyway?"

"Green Tourmaline. It's not the most valuable in the world, but worth a lot more than a couple hundred dollars."

I turned and looked at Alex. A glass display case caught my eye, displaying various colors and shapes of gems or stones. "What's the green tourmaline worth?"

Julie paused for a moment. "The piece the gentleman had with him? About seven thousand dollars."

"Oh," I said.

I looked down at Annie—the old woman—as she appeared to be listening but kept her gaze down on what she was doing. "That's the last time you saw Charles?" I said.

"It's the last time he was involved in anything that had to do with us."

"Do you have any information on him? An old membership file or something to help us find him?"

"Can't you just go to where he lives?"

"That's the problem," I said. "I don't know where he is. And his ex-wife doesn't seem to know, either."

I looked out of the corner of my eye at the old woman. Something was odd about her but I couldn't quite put my finger on it.

Julie gestured for us to follow her, turned and walked down a short hall and into another room. There were shelves filled with figures and sculptures and shiny things I knew nothing about. She sat down behind an old, wooden desk. There was no computer or any sign of anything modern in the room, which I guessed was her office.

Julie reached down behind her desk and pulled open a drawer. She came up with a stack of folders and tossed them in front of me. "His membership information should be in here." She flipped through the papers inside one of the folders. "Here," she said, and handed me a sheet of paper.

I said, "Is this his address?"

She shrugged. "It's what he listed as his business address. It's from a year ago, I don't know if he still has the business. Word is he's not the most honest man. And in a community like ours..." She stood from her desk and walked out the door.

Alex and I followed her back into the front room.

Julie turned to us as we came up behind her. "I'll keep you in mind if we ever need a Private Investigator. As you might guess, there are a lot of unscrupulous people in the industry. A lot goes on, and the cops don't always make it a priority to help us."

I reached for the door, turned to Julie and said, "Did Charles ever talk to anyone about an artist in France, a man by the name of Francois de Pierre?"

Julie shrugged. "I never knew what to believe when Charles opened his mouth, if his so-called contacts were nothing more than a figment of his imagination. Or a way to con anyone who wasn't aware of his shady tactics."

I said, "Francois de Pierre created a sculpture that Charles was supposed to sell for him. I've never seen it and know little about it other than it's a pelican made of expensive crystal."

Julie stood quiet for a moment as she looked off toward the back of the room. She began to shake her head. "I'm sorry, I don't know if I can help you any further."

I watched her, wondering what she was holding back. There was something. Even the old woman at the table seemed a bit odd, paying much more attention to the conversation than she would let on.

Chapter 19

WE DROVE PAST THE sign for the St. Johns Industrial Park as we entered what looked like an abandoned road. It was narrow with overgrown trees on either side and busted asphalt covered in foot-high weeds. If a car came the other way, one of us would have had to pull off the so-called road.

My leg felt better, so I was back behind the wheel of my new but well-aged Lexus. I turned to Alex in the passenger seat. "Guess these businesses didn't get the message? Location, location, location. Isn't that what they say?"

She nodded. "Weird place. Certainly off the beaten path. You sure this is it?" She looked down at her phone. "It says we've arrived. But I can't see how that's possible."

Many of the large brick buildings appeared vacant, with large paper signs taped to the inside of the windows advertising space available.

I stopped in front of the door where the number one-oh-eight was stuck on in gold and black lettering. I pulled the paper from my pocket and read the address. "This is it."

I leaned over the steering wheel looking toward the store front, trying to see inside. To my left were two parked cars, but otherwise it looked like the apocalypse had already hit this particular development.

Under the number one-oh-eight was a white piece of paper with WE PAY CASH printed in all capital letters. I looked toward Alex as we both stepped out of the car. An OPEN sign hung from a hook on the glass, although I wasn't sure that was accurate. As we walked to the door, I saw another sign written by hand in black magic marker:

BY APPOINTMENT ONLY.

I pulled on the door, expecting it to be locked. But it wasn't. I held it for Alex and walked in behind her. The fluorescent light was dim but the sun came in from the windows and brightened the front of the space.

"Hello?" I said, looking toward a doorway behind a glass display case with a small cash register on top. There was a curtain across the doorway, hanging halfway down to the floor.

Whistling came from the back of the place.

Alex and I exchanged looks as she straightened out the holster under her shirt.

A man walked through the doorway behind the counter with his head down, looking at something he held in his hand.

He jumped back when he saw us. "Jesus Christ," he said. "How'd you get in here?"

I pointed behind me with my thumb "The door was unlocked."

The man was short, a bit on the heavy side, with white hair although a lot missing on top. A pair of reading glasses sat toward the end of his nose.

He squinted, looking over his glasses at me. "Something I can help you with?"

I stepped toward the display case he was standing behind. "Are you Charles?"

He scratched the bald part of his head. "I'm Charles." He removed the glasses from the edge of his nose and placed them down on the counter. He looked right at Alex, and a smile filled his face. "Normally I'm only open by appointment." He shrugged. "But a beautiful woman comes in my place, last thing I'm going to do is turn her away." He leaned on the glass display's top and looked down toward the floor. His gaze moved up Alex's legs before he turned to me. "Sir, I don't have any diamonds right now. But if I were you, I'd get a ring on this lady's finger as soon as you can. Let her get away, you'll never forgive yourself."

I turned and smiled at Alex.

She rolled her eyes.

A man close to my size but taller and heavier walked through the front door. Dressed in black, head-to-toe, he wore a shiny, fancy t-shirt that was at least a couple of sizes too small, barely covering the fat hanging over his belt. He pushed his chest out, hung his arms behind him, doing his best to look like he was in better shape than he actually was.

Charles watched as he walked past him, "Where've you been?"

The man walked behind the display case, reached up and pushed the curtain to one side of the doorway. He disappeared into the back for a moment, came back out with a bag of chips and a magazine in his hand.

Charles said to him, "You left the door unlocked."

The man took a seat on a stool behind the display case, stuffing his mouth with chips. "Did I?" He opened the magazine and started flipping through the pages.

Charles let out a sigh, turned back to me and Alex and said, "Could you at least tell me your names?"

The man behind the counter lifted his head from the magazine, watching us.

"I'm Henry Walsh. This is Alex. Alex Jepson."

Charles looked at the man behind the display case. "This is Dominic."

"Dominic?" I looked back at him. "You look familiar. You from around here?"

He shook his head. "Nope." He looked down at the magazine.

Charles said, "Dominic kind of watches over the place... keeps an eye on things." He raised his eyebrows and cracked a grin. "That includes me."

"What includes you?" I said.

"Dominic. He keeps me out of trouble."

"Oh," I said.

"I get the feeling you're not here as a buyer?" Charles said.

I shook my head. "I'm here about a friend of yours...a business associate."

"Oh yeah? Who might that be?"

"Philip Wetzel."

Charles turned, glanced back at Dominic, then walked around to the front of the display case. "You a cop?" he said.

"No, just a friend of Philip's."

Charles stood in front of me with his arms folded. "It's hard to believe what happened to him."

119

"You mean that someone killed him? Or that his fiancé's been kidnapped?" I said.

"His fiancé? I didn't know she—"

"She's missing. And we still don't know if Philip's dead or alive."

"I didn't hear anything. I mean...I only heard what they said on the news. They didn't mention his fiancé."

"You know her?" I said.

Charles shook his head. "Never met her."

"She disappeared the morning of the explosion." I glared back at Dominic. There was something about him and the way he snuck a peak at me every time he flipped a page in the magazine. But I couldn't place his face. I wondered if he had any connection to my mishap in Neptune Beach. He looked the type. Although, the truth was he looked like every other New York transplant who dressed like a hitman on a picnic.

Charles looked past me, out toward the windows at the front of his space. "So, what is it you need from me?"

"For starters, I'm wondering if you could tell me if you've ever rented a car from Darcy Car Rental."

"I've heard of it. But, no, I've never been there."

I gave Charles my best look to let him know I smelled BS. "You're telling me you've never rented a car from Darcy Car Rental?"

He raised his eyebrows high up on his forehead. "I'm telling you the truth. Never have. At least not that I remember."

I held my hand up to him, my palm a foot from his face. I looked at my watch. "In just over twenty-seconds, you went from never renting a car there...to not remembering if you rented a car there." I glanced back at Alex and pulled a copy of the invoice from my pocket. "Here." I handed him the paper. "Is that your name on this invoice?"

Charles pushed his glasses up on his face and looked at the invoice. "C. Weiss?" He looked over the paper. "This wasn't me. It doesn't even say Charles. And I'm not the only Weiss with a C as the first initial, you know."

"I already talked to your wife. She claims to know as much as you do about it." I glanced at Dominic. "And it just so happens, after I left Carla's apartment a car followed me a few minutes after I walked out of a bar called Skips. Two guys jumped out and one of them shot me." I pointed to my thigh, "Right here in the leg."

Charles shrugged.

"So what can you tell me about the crystal pelican?" I said.

Charles shifted his stance, his gaze back on Dominic for a moment, then back at me. "Where'd you hear about that?" He gave me some dumb look, his mouth hung open like his brain had locked up.

"I know about the deal you set up with Philip's father. I know about the artist over there in France. And I know about Frank..."

"Frank? Philip's brother? What's he got to do with any of this? Guy's a small-time crook. Nothing but a two-bit—"

"You didn't partner with Frank, hoping to get the sculpture back after Philip's father died?"

Charles stared back at me, frozen for a moment. "I swear. I had nothing to do with what happened."

I kept quiet, knowing Charles seemed to be the type who'd keep talking when there was silence in the air. "I mean, if I'm being honest, of course I'd like to know what happened to that pelican. But killing Philip wouldn't get me anywhere. In fact I'd met with him a few times, seeing what kind of a deal we could work out. But he didn't know where it was. He said he'd do what he could to help find it. Obviously, he wouldn't be much help to me if he was dead."

I said, "I don't know. Maybe you kidnapped Victoria, threatened him...told him she'll be dead if he doesn't hand it over. Then we have a different story, don't we?"

I turned to Dominic. "What about you? What's your role in all this?"

Dominic put his magazine down on the glass display case in front of him and folded his arms at his chest. He stared back at me and didn't say a word.

He got up from the stool and came around to our side. "Listen. I don't know what your deal is or who you think you are. I know you're not a cop, but—"

"I'm a private investigator," I said as Dominic approached me.

"Henry, let me explain something," Charles said. "I spent quite a few years in France. I built relationships with all these artists who thought they shit ice cream. They wouldn't give most people the time of day, but I pulled it off. I pulled together a deal with Philip's father, Mr. Wetzel. And when he died, it all kind of fell apart. But I'd already delivered my end of the deal. And Philip—he promised to help me locate the sculpture and get me the money I was owed. You see what I'm saying?"

I shook my head. "Actually, no."

"I owe him a lot of money."

"Who?"

"Francois De Pierre. He's the artist. He knows a lot of people, and if I don't find that sculpture or at least get my cut, Francois doesn't get his money. And I don't know what'll happen to me. But, right now, I'm always looking over my shoulder." He pointed with his thumb toward Dominic. "You think I can afford to pay this guy as much as I do? Like I said, he keeps an eye on things. He makes sure I don't get plugged until I either find the sculpture or someone pays me."

"You mean when Philip pays you?"

Charles shrugged. "He swears he doesn't know where his father stored it." I noticed a sticker on the wall that said, *Member, Jacksonville Gem and Mineral Society.*

"You oughta take that bumper sticker down off your wall."

Charles followed my eyes, then turned to me with a stupid look on his face. "What?"

"I stopped there looking for you. I was told you weren't welcome there any longer."

Charles rolled his eyes. "What'd she tell you? Whatever it was, trust me...it's all a lie to keep me out of there. They were intimidated by me, that's all."

I heard you tried to rip off an old man."

Charles shook his head and brushed his hand through the air. "This man comes up to me at a show. I'm doing the appraisals, okay? This man—about eighty years old—he comes up, asked me about this green tourmaline he's got in this little box. He asked if I wanted to buy it. I told him I wasn't supposed to be buying, only offering the free appraisals. So I said the most I'd give him was a few hundred bucks. I mean, the guy sounded like he needed some money. Said it was his dead wife's piece. Then this old hag—she's one of the members on the board—she starts barking at me, said I was trying to rip off the other members."

Alex and I exchanged looks.

I thought for a moment. "So who else knows about this pelican?"

Charles cocked his head back. "Who knows about it? Who doesn't?"

Chapter 20

ALEX AND I SAT at a table on the patio having drinks outside the Bayside Grille, overlooking the St. Johns. I called Philip, but the call didn't go through, the message saying the number was not in service.

"Burner phone," I said as I ended the call. "Wouldn't surprise me, he uses a different phone every time he makes a call." I looked out toward the river. "I just hope he calls so I can get some answers from him."

"Charles seemed to be hiding something," Alex said.

"So didn't Dominic. And his ex-wife, Carla."

Alex said, "What about Frank and his young friend? Where do they come in?"

We both sat quiet for a moment.

I turned to her. "Have you heard anything else about that girl from Darcy Rental?"

Alex shook her head. "No, nothing. Mike said he'd let me know once he had some information."

"No leads?"

"He said it could've been anything. Someone looking for some drug money."

I said, "You mean she happened to be in the wrong place at the wrong time?" I shook my head. "I don't think so."

Alex took a sip from her bottle of beer. "He doesn't think it's related to any of this, if that's what you're getting at."

The waitress came by with our lunch and put the plates down on the table.

I looked at the screen on my phone. "I wonder when he's going to call?"

"Philip?" Alex said. "Don't you think he's trying to find Victoria?"

"I'm sure he is. But he also gave me quite a bit of money to help him. You'd think he'd at least call." I slid the phone back in my pocket just as it started to buzz. I looked at the screen but didn't recognize the number. "Walsh Investigations," I said.

"Henry Walsh?"

"This is him."

"You want to keep Victoria alive, you find the pelican."

I straightened out in my seat. "Who is this?"

"You don't get that sculpture within forty-eight hours, I'll be sure to let Philip know Victoria's death was your fault."

The call disconnected. I looked at Alex without saying a word as I slipped the phone back into my pocket.

"What's wrong?" Alex said.

"I don't know. But whoever it was, claimed he had Victoria. He said we have two days to get him the sculpture, or else she'll die."

"The sculpture?"

"The pelican." I looked down at the food I'd yet to touch. "Someone obviously knows every step I make. Probably watched us meet with Philip."

Alex said, "You don't think it was Charles...trying to get what he believes is his?"

I shrugged. "Could be any number of people at this point. Especially his ex. Can't imagine it was just a coincidence, someone tracks me down and shoots me after I left her apartment."

Alex took a bite of her sandwich.

"In hindsight, I wish I'd gotten in the car with them when they told me to. Not only could I've avoided getting shot, but I'd know who we're dealing with."

Alex wiped her mouth and gave me a look. "That's foolish. You'd be dead."

"No, I wouldn't have been dead. Not if they were hoping I'd lead them to Philip."

"Oh. Right. So you'd both be dead."

The waitress came back to our table and put two drinks down in front of us. We'd barely touched the ones we already had.

"Thank you," I said as I looked up at the waitress. "But we didn't order these."

The waitress turned and looked over her shoulder toward the patio bar on the other side of the patio.

There was a woman sitting alone in a long, white sundress and a wide, flowered sun hat. She turned toward us and smiled. She held her dark sunglasses down just a little off her eyes.

The waitress nodded toward the woman. "They're from her."

The woman raised her glass to us as Alex and I both stared back at her.

But then I realized who it was. I got up and walked toward the bar where she sat.

Alex said, "Henry?" But I kept walking.

The woman in the white sun dress stood from her stool as I approached her and held out her arms. She wrapped them around my neck and pulled me toward her. "Oh, Henry."

"Kathleen? What...what are you doing here? How'd you—"

"Aren't you going to thank me for the drinks?" She gave me a crooked smile...the same one I'd gotten to know for the few weeks I'd spent with her on Ocracoke Island out on the Outer Banks.

She held onto both of my hands and looked me up and down. "You look as good as I remember." She looked down at my bandaged leg. "Are you okay?"

I nodded and looked toward Alex, still seated, sipping her beer.

"Who is your friend?" she said.

"Come on, I'll introduce you."

She followed me over to Alex.

"Alex," I said. "This is Kathleen."

Alex wiped her hands with her napkin and stood up from the table. She looked at Kathleen, shook her hand, then looked back at me with a curious look.

"Kathleen. You know, from Ocracoke?"

Alex nodded.

Kathleen said to her, "I've heard a lot about you."

Right after I'd left my job as Director of Security for the Jacksonville Sharks baseball team—and after I helped solve Lance Moreau's murder—I knew I needed a little break from Florida.

Or, a break from reality.

The team had paid me well enough for the investigation, even though I was also their Director of Security. So I had some extra cash and traveled north to Ocracoke Island with a plan to relax for a couple of weeks.

But then I met Kathleen, who approached me out of the blue one night at a local bar right on Silver Lake.

She'd told me at the time she'd been there to have a little fun. And, for the most part, that was my intent too.

So fun is what we had. At least until I woke up one morning to a note on the refrigerator from Kathleen that said she'd gone home. The thing was, I knew she'd at one time lived in New York, but not much else. I never got her phone number. Never knew her last name. When she disappeared from the island, I was left with nothing more than an empty wallet.

I turned to Kathleen, "What are you doing in Florida?"

She pushed her sunglasses up onto her head. "I knew the way I left Ocracoke was wrong. And I've felt bad about it ever since. So I looked you up and, well..." She put on a big smile. "Here I am!"

Alex knew the whole story about Ocracoke and how Kathleen left me high and dry. She wasn't about to sugar coat her feelings toward her. "So, does that mean you followed us here?"

Kathleen's smile faded as she looked down toward the ground. "I know it was wrong of me to do what I did, it's just—"

I brushed my hand through the air. "No, really. It's fine. No need to..." I stopped, then hesitated a moment. "It's good to see you."

I'd forgotten how attractive she was.

Alex gave me a look, one like as if she'd smelled low tide. "I'm sorry, but you didn't answer me. Have you been following us?"

I swallowed. I wondered for a moment if I'd have to step between them. I turned to Alex. "It's fine. Really. It's not a big deal."

But Kathleen looked Alex in the eye. "I stopped at Billy's Place. Henry had told me about it. I knew he was friends with the owner. So I went there." She glanced back at me with a smile. "He said you'd be here." She pulled her glasses back down over her eyes.

The three of us were quiet for a moment.

"Okay, well I'll let you two finish your lunch." She turned and started to walk away.

I turned to Alex, "Give me a minute, okay?"

Alex gave me a look and sat back down at the table.

I followed Kathleen as she stood at the bar and grabbed her credit card from the bartender and slipped it inside her purse. She snapped the top closed with her long fingers. "I didn't mean to intrude, you know." She leaned over and kissed me on the cheek. "I'll call you later."

"You have my number?"

She nodded. "Billy gave it to me. But I thought I'd surprise you." Kathleen turned and walked across the patio and through a glass door. She disappeared inside the restaurant.

I walked back to the table and sat down across from Alex.

"She seems, uh, nice?" she said as she rolled her eyes.

I sipped my drink. "Weird, she'd come down to Florida out of the blue to find me." I pushed my untouched plate of food to the side.

130

"Weird," Alex said. "To put it mildly."

Chapter 21

WITH MY LEG FINALLY feeling a little better, I made myself at home again upstairs at Billy's Place. I had a bathroom with a shower, a desk, a couch to sleep on, and a restaurant with a full bar downstairs.

What more did I need?

I made my way down to the bar. Billy slid a glass in front of me and poured me a Jack Daniels with two cubes. The thing about Billy was he understood how to pour a drink. You'd think any bartender could give me a simple Jack with two cubes. But most—if not all—would pour Old Number 7 over a full glass of ice, even after I'd said, "Just two cubes." Not a glass full of cubes that'd turn my drink into Kentucky-whiskey flavored water. Not even four cubes. Two. That's all I asked, but few bartenders could do the math.

"Where'd you find that shirt?" Billy said, his hands on his hips, looking down at me in my stool.

"Why? Do you like it?" I said.

"Short sleeves and buttons? And a cute little pocket for your pencils?"

"It's all I have."

"All you have? I wouldn't say you're the sharpest dresser, but you usually do a little better than coming down dressed like a school boy." Billy shrugged. "I don't know. Maybe it's fine." He leaned on the counter, both hands spread out wide in front of him. "You heading out for the night?"

I sipped my Jack. "You remember the woman from Ocra-coke?"

"The good looking one, was in here earlier looking for you?" I looked at my watch and nodded. "I'm meeting her out for a couple of drinks."

"Just to refresh my memory...she left you high-and-dry out in Ocracoke with a pretty hefty bar bill. Is that the one?"

"Yeah, that's the one."

"But I could see what you're thinking. With looks like that, I'd give her a few extra chances." Billy looked at my shirt. "Well, then on second thought, not a bad idea you find something else to wear. You show up in that thing, might be the second time she ditches you." Billy looked over his shoulder, pulled two wine glasses down from the rack overhead and filled them with red wine.

"Give me a minute," he said, and delivered drinks to two very attractive women. I heard Billy ask them what they thought of my shirt. The three of them looked my way, the two women shrugged.

Billy walked back over.

"No. The shirt's fine." He sipped from a glass bottle of Perrier. "You tell Alex you had a date?"

"I was out with her, having lunch, when Kathleen showed up."

"Was that a little uncomfortable?"

"Why?"

Billy looked down at me. "For someone so perceptive, you have trouble seeing what's right in front of you."

I sipped my Jack and looked up at him over the glass, waiting for him to say more.

"She stopped in a little while ago."

"Alex?"

Billy nodded, wiping the inside of a glass with his towel. "She was pretty upset." He waved his hand at me. "I don't mean she was crying. Not Alex. But she was, I guess...pretty annoyed you'd give this woman the time of day."

"So what're you saying?"

Billy shrugged. "Alex thinks a lot of you. I guess you know that. But sometimes...I don't know what I'm trying to say, it's just..."

Billy didn't finish.

I shot back what remained in my glass and stood up from my stool. I threw a bill down on the bar. "Alex and I have been through it all before."

• • • ● • ● • • •

Kathleen was already at the Sand Dollar, waiting for me at the bar. She sipped from a wine glass and waved for me as I walked through the door.

She stood from her seat and gave me a hug as I approached, then held onto my hand for a moment longer as we pulled apart from each other.

I took the seat next to her at the bar.

"I love your shirt," she said.

"Oh, thanks. I don't have much left. Lost some of my things. I don't know if you heard about what happened?"

She shook her head. "Happened to what?"

"Remember me telling you about the boat I lived on? The one my friend Philip owned?"

"Philip? He was the one who owned the house you stayed in?"

"Yes, that's him."

"Is everything all right?"

I waved down the bartender and ordered a Jack Daniels with two pieces of ice.

"You want it on the rocks?" he said.

"I want it neat. But with two cubes."

He stared back at me for a moment, turned and reached for a glass.

"Philip is missing. He was on the boat—the one I used to live on—and there was an explosion. As unbelievable as that may sound."

She said, "He's alive?"

Even though I figured I could trust Kathleen, I didn't think it'd make any sense to let her know the full story. I paused for a moment. "They haven't been able to find him or his body. But right now, it's likely he didn't survive."

Kathleen put her hand over her open mouth. "Oh, Henry. I'm so sorry."

The bartender slid my glass in front of me. Sure enough, I got a Jack Daniels on the rocks, more ice than whisky. I grabbed a spoon and scooped the ice from the glass and left it on top of a cocktail napkin. The bartender walked by and I said, "Here are the extra cubes I don't need."

Kathleen and I reminisced about the time we'd spent together on Ocracoke. Most of it was somewhat hard to remember, since we spent most days with a drink in our hands.

Her knees touched my legs as I turned in my seat to face her. I looked past her for a moment, out toward the Saint Johns.

"Are you okay?" she said. She put her hand on my leg.

I looked down and noticed a white line on the skin of her ring finger. It seemed to be the only part of her body that wasn't tan. Although it was hard to say for sure, being that she was fully clothed.

I put my drink down on the bar. "So what is it you're really doing here? I'm flattered if you came all the way here to see me. But I'm not sure I buy it."

My question hung in the air.

She looked down into her glass of wine, moved closer to me in her stool, her bare knees pressed up against my thigh. "I was married when we met." She looked at me with a deep stare, like she was trying to find my soul somewhere behind my eyes. She again put her hand on my leg. "I'm sorry I didn't tell you. That's why I had to leave."

"Married, huh?" I nodded, turning toward the bar. "I guess I should've asked."

She shrugged. "Why?"

"It crossed my mind. You snuck away to make those phone calls. I was like a middle-school boy, the way I acted. I told you everything about me. Too much, maybe. And you told me nothing about you."

"You didn't ask."

I raised my eyebrows. "I even noticed you had a little white on your ring finger. Like you do right now. So you could say I knew, but chose to ignore it."

I finished my drink in one straight shot and pushed my glass toward the far edge of the bar. The bartender came by and held up the bottle of Jack. I gave him a nod. "Make it a double. Neat this time with rocks on the side."

Kathleen continued. "We weren't together when I was with you."

"You weren't together? But you went home to him, didn't you?"

She nodded as she looked away. "He begged me to come home. We tried to make it work." She looked down into her glass, quiet for a moment. "I never stopped thinking of you."

The bartender poured my drink, put the glass of rocks down in front of me and brought Kathleen another glass of white wine.

"Did he know about me?"

Kathleen closed her eyes. With both hands on her glass, down on the bar in front of her, she nodded.

"And now? Are you back together?"

She shook her head, still quiet as she looked down toward the floor. "We're separated."

· · · ● · ● · · ·

After a few drinks with Kathleen, I drove out to see Alex and parked behind her Jeep.

As I walked up the walkway toward her porch, her dog Raz let out a loud bark from behind the window. But then he whimpered as he saw it was me.

Alex opened the door with a bottle of beer in each hand and handed me one as she stepped out onto the porch. Raz ran out past her, foregoing his normal crotch greeting to instead sniff my wounded leg.

"How was the date?" Alex said.

I gave her a quick glance but didn't answer her. Not right away.

We both sat down on the top step, both of us quiet for a moment. Raz sat between us, his head rested on his big paws hanging over the edge.

"It wasn't a date," I said.

"Just catching up with someone who was such a big part of your life?" She sipped her beer, gazing at me from over the bottle. "Remind me again...how many hours did you know her?"

I turned and gave her a look. "I've never seen you like this before."

"Like what?"

"Jealous. It's not like you."

Alex pushed me away from her and got up from the stair. "Don't flatter yourself." She walked through the door and went inside.

I looked down at Raz and rubbed the top of his big head. "I don't know what to tell you, Raz." He looked up at me, turned his head as much as he could to look toward the door, then put his head back down on top of his paws.

Alex came back out onto the porch and cracked the cap off another beer. She sat down again on the top step next to Raz.

"What if those men who came after me had something to do with Kathleen?" I said. "What if it had nothing to do with Philip?"

"You mean someone's after you?" Alex shrugged.

I waited a moment. "Kathleen was married."

Alex acted surprised, her mouth wide open. "Really? No way." She laughed. "First thing I noticed was the white band of skin on her ring finger."

Chapter 22

I SAT IN THE waiting room of the visitor's area at the John E. Goode Pretrial Detention Facility or the PDF, as it was better known. A guard called my name and led me to a cold, empty room with a long table and a chair on either side.

I sat down in one of the chairs as the door opened behind me. A guard walked in and sat Philip's brother Frank down in the chair across from me.

The guard left the room and peaked in through the small window in the door he'd closed behind him.

Frank kept his stare on me for a moment, not saying a word.

I gave him a friendly nod. "Hello, Frank."

"What the hell are you doing here?" he said.

"I thought you could use a visitor. Someone to talk to." I looked around the empty room. "Can't imagine you have visitors lined up to see you."

He dropped his eyelids halfway down over his eyes. "You the one who got me pinched?"

I slowly shook my head. "The neighbor you stole the car from had no trouble telling the sheriff's office who stole her car." I shrugged. "Although I will admit I encouraged her to make the call."

He stared back at me, folded his arms at his chest. "What the hell do you want with me?"

I leaned forward on the table, my hands folded in front of my chin. I looked past Frank toward the guard behind the door. "I almost forgot, with so much going on, that you'd pulled a gun on me. I'm sure that'd go over well, tacked on top of an auto theft and assault charge." I shrugged. "Maybe I should bring that up with someone?"

"I gave the car back to her that night. Even apologized. I simply borrowed it."

I huffed out a laugh. "I'm sure the Judge'll buy that one."

"You're not a cop. And you're not my lawyer. I have nothing to say to you."

"For starters, how about you tell me why you came after me?"

Frank took a deep breath, the veins in his neck thick as the pressure seemed to build inside him. "I was looking for my brother. Nothing more to it than that."

"You ever think to, uh, I don't know...maybe just ask me? Without the threat of shooting led through my skull?"

Frank turned and looked over his shoulder toward the door. "Keep your voice down, will you?"

"So why, after all these years, are you suddenly down here looking for Philip?"

"Because I need his help."

"*You* need his help?" I leaned back in the chair and scratched my chin for nothing more than effect. "You know the sheriff's office is saying Philip's most likely dead, right?"

"Presumed dead," Frank said.

"That's correct," I said.

"Philip spent just about as much time in the oceans around the world as he has on land."

I didn't break my stare. "And?"

"I'd bet he's alive. And I'd bet he's hiding. I wouldn't put it past him...he blew up that boat all by himself. Just so he could hide."

I leaned forward on the table again, as close as I could get to Frank without leaving my seat. "Would you bet the crystal pelican?"

He stared back at me, his chin up. He took a moment before he spoke. "What do *you* know about that?"

"Not much, to be honest. But I get the feeling someone out there wants to get his or her hands on it. Maybe bad enough to kidnap Victoria and try to kill Philip."

"Who've you talked to?" Frank said.

I looked back toward the guard behind the small window on the door. He was laughing with another guard, barely paying attention. "Doesn't matter who. But I do understand it's worth quite a bit of money."

Frank shifted in the chair and leaned forward on the table. "It disappeared after my father died. There was a deal in place with this dealer, and..."

"Charles Weiss?"

Frank raised his eyebrows. "You know him?"

"He's someone I've come across."

"Well, nobody seemed to know where it ended up. I assumed Philip had it, or maybe even hid it. But, to be honest, we weren't the closest of brothers. Especially over the past few years. It's not like he'd tell me."

We both sat quiet for a moment.

"So what's your deal, anyway?" Frank said.

"My deal?"

"You workin' for Philip?"

I shook my head.

"You're a private detective, right?"

"Private investigator."

"But you're not working for Philip? Then why are you involved? Who hired you to come here and crawl up my ass."

I folded my arms and stared at Frank across the table. "Who I work for is none of your business. The fact is, you pulled a gun on me. Then I showed up at your door and you ran. Which, coincidentally, is what got you in here in the first place." I stood up and looked down at Frank. "Philip was my friend. And that boat was my home for the past three years. It could've just as easily been me on there when that bomb went off. And if you or anyone you're friendly with has anything to do with planting that bomb or taking Victoria, I'll see to it myself...you'll go down hard. That might mean behind bars...or the wrong side of the ground."

I headed for the door.

"Wait," Frank said.

I stopped and turned to him.

"What if I was willing to help you? How about...you help me, I help you?"

I looked back toward the door, ready to walk away rather than listen to what kind of deal Frank wanted to negotiate.

"You said you talked to Charles Weiss, right?"

I took a couple of steps toward Frank and nodded. "Why?"

"I don't know what he told you—if you did talk to him—but that deal he had with my father...the whole thing almost got called off."

"What do you mean?"

"My father didn't trust him, didn't think he'd come through on what he'd promised."

I looked at Frank. "Is that why Charles went to you?"

"You don't miss a beat, huh?" He looked toward the door.

"So, what, you help Charles pull off the deal with your father, he cuts you in on a share?"

Frank nodded as the guard walked in, said the visitation was over, and dragged Frank out the door ahead of me.

• • • ● • ● • • •

I sat at the bar for a quick drink but to also talk to Billy. He was one of those people you could talk to. And he'd actually listen. And when asked—only when asked—he'd give you his advice. And it was usually pretty good.

"Didn't see you upstairs this morning," he said as he poured Jack into my glass.

"Just got back from the detention center," I said. "Philip's brother Frank got arrested for stealing his neighbor's car."

"He stole his neighbor's car?"

I nodded. "He used the word 'borrowed' but that's not the way I saw it. The judge won't see it that way either, unless the woman decides to drop the charges for some reason." I sipped my drink. "He did it right in front of me, so I could help put him away for a bit if I wanted to."

"Why wouldn't you?"

"I went there to see what he knows about Philip. And about this clown Charles Weiss."

"Frank's the one who pulled the gun on you?"

I had my glass up under my mouth. "Yeah, that was Frank."

Billy poured four drafts of beer from the tap, held all four mugs together and carried them across the bar without spilling a drop.

He walked back over and leaned with his hands down on the bar in front of me. "But he's not the one who shot you?"

"I don't think so."

"No leads yet on who did?"

I shook my head. "Not yet."

Billy crouched down behind the bar and came up with an unopened bottle of Jack, cracked the top and put it up on the shelf behind the bar. "Did you meet your friend last night?" he said.

"Kathleen?" I nodded. "She's married."

"Oh."

I lifted my glass. "Separated, I guess. But her husband knows about me."

"She said that?"

I nodded. "Alex thinks I'm being paranoid, but there's a little part of me wondering if this had something to do with me being shot."

"You mean, it might not be connected to Philip?" Billy tilted his head a bit. "Really?"

"I don't know," I said. "I was sure it had to do with Philip. I mean, why would the husband show up in Neptune Beach? It's not like I'm ever out there..."

Billy said, "I'd have to side with Alex. You're being paranoid."

"Then the boat blows up," I said. "So, of course, I start to wonder, maybe—"

"Henry, they kidnapped his fiancé. Are you trying to say the explosion's not related?"

I said, "A coincidence?"

Billy pulled the towel from over his shoulder and wiped out the glasses he pulled from the dishwasher behind the bar. He nodded toward my empty glass. "Another?"

I pushed my glass forward.

Chloe—Billy's most loyal employee who he considers family—walked in from the kitchen, tying her smock around her waist. "Sorry I'm late," she said, seeming out of breath. "Hey Henry." She gave me a big smile.

Chloe had recently graduated from college, but kept working for Billy. She was smart. But like Billy, she enjoyed being behind the bar. It didn't hurt that her boyfriend, Jake, was in charge of the kitchen.

"Henry, someone was in here looking for you a couple of days ago. Didn't know where you were, and wouldn't have told him if I did."

"Him?"

She nodded.

Billy and I looked at each other.

"You get a name?" I said.

"No. And he wasn't very friendly."

"What'd he look like?"

She shrugged. "I don't know. Dark hair. A little heavy, wore a black t-shirt, black pants. Had a chain on his neck that matched his thick gold watch."

Billy leaned toward me, just over the bar. "The husband?"

Chloe threw up her hands and covered her ears. "I don't want to know a thing." She walked away, started chatting with one of the older couples down the bar.

Billy dropped two cubes in my glass and poured a shot of Jack over the top. "Any idea?"

"This guy Charles Weiss...he's the one involved with Philip or Philip's father...maybe Frank, too. Well, he has this guy working for him. A bodyguard, I guess. Didn't talk much, but sounds like someone Chloe just described."

Chapter 23

I SAT ON A park bench at Friendship Fountain, on the lookout for a bearded man with a baseball hat and sunglasses. Philip had finally called, and I asked him to meet me there so he could answer some questions. He was hesitant at first, but finally agreed to meet.

But I'd already waited twenty minutes, and saw no sign of him anywhere. I looked at my watch and started to think maybe something happened to him.

The probability of that seemed to be increasing.

It was a pretty busy area. I watched the younger women and maybe one or two men pushing kids in strollers around the fountain. The older kids ran around as their moms tried to keep up without taking their heads out of their phones. There were runners and walkers, people of all ages. Three old ladies sat together on a park bench not far from me, talking to each other as they seemed relaxed, staring at the fountain.

I felt a hand on my shoulder that I think startled me a bit. More than it normally would.

It was Philip.

"Where've you been?" I said as I looked at my watch. "I was starting to wonder..."

Philip looked down at me, quiet for a moment. "I went to my brother's apartment. I thought I could talk to him, maybe see what he knows, but...there was some kid there. His name was Jayray or Rayjay or something. The kid answered the door, said Frank had been arrested."

"He's at the John E. Goode Pretrial Detention Facility," I said as I stood up off the bench.

"Frank?"

I nodded.

"You knew he'd been arrested?"

"Not sure it's going to hold. He returned the car. And the value's barely five hundred dollars. Looking at a misdemeanor."

I didn't tell Philip the whole story or mention I was there when Frank took the woman's car.

"But, what I don't understand," I said, "is why you'd risk going to his apartment?"

Philip looked off for a moment and removed his sunglasses from his face. "He is my brother. I hoped he'd know something about Victoria. Be willing to talk to me."

"You're walking around here in a fake beard and that ugly baseball hat—like a homeless person—so nobody'll recognize you? But then you're out and about, knocking on doors?" I said. "Why bother with the disguise?"

"Well, he wasn't there anyway, obviously. And the kid—"

"Jayray?"

"Yeah, he's not one for conversation. Didn't say much."

I gestured for Philip to follow me. "I'd rather not be a sitting duck. I get the feeling you're not fooling anyone."

We started walking along the walk around the fountain. I said, "Do you owe Charles Weiss money for that crystal pelican?"

He didn't answer my question directly. "You talked to Charles?"

"I went to his shop. Told me he owes the artist who created the sculpture. And he's afraid if he doesn't pay him..."

Philip shook his head. "Don't let him fool you. He's not in any danger."

"What makes you so sure?"

Philip stared straight ahead without answering.

"He hired a bodyguard," I said.

"Did he?" Philip stopped and faced me. "Charles dealt with my father. It had nothing to do with me." He started walking ahead of me. "Did you speak with Carla Weiss?"

I picked up my pace and followed behind. "I did."

"She plays it cool, doesn't she? Smokes her weed, lets on like she doesn't know which end is up or down." He stopped and turned to me, wagged his finger. "But that couldn't be further from the truth." He again picked up the pace and walked ahead of me. "I gotta go, Henry."

"Go where? You said you'd meet me. How am I supposed to find Victoria if you won't even take the time to tell me what I need to know?"

I followed him across the grass as he headed back toward the street. I said, "Philip, do you remember that woman I met in Ocracoke last year?"

He nodded. "Of course." He paused for a moment. "The one who left you, without saying a word?"

"Yes, that's her. For some reason, she's here in Florida. Showed up out of the blue, said she'd been looking for me."

"Good for you," he said, and started walking again. I picked up my pace and walked alongside him. "Turns out she was married."

"Yeah?"

"Still might be," I said.

"Don't take this the wrong way, Henry. I don't know if you're looking for advice or something or just making small talk, but if this doesn't have anything to do with Victoria..."

"She said her husband knew she was with me. Couldn't have been very happy."

Philip stopped again. "And?..."

"Well, I was thinking. What if the bomb wasn't meant for you? What if her husband—and I have no idea who this guy is—what if he thought I was on that boat?"

"And he calls me? Takes my fiancé from me?" Philip shook his head. "You're beginning to sound crazy."

"Am I? How many people actually knew you were living on that boat? Not many, right? Did your brother know? Did Charles?"

Philip paused. "I don't know. I guess I didn't tell many people."

"And what about those three men who came after me? What if it had nothing to do with you?"

"You think they kidnapped Victoria because you were screwing someone's wife?"

151

I shook my head. "No, what I'm saying is, maybe the two are unrelated." I thought for a moment. "And I didn't know she was married."

Philip continued ahead of me and finally reached his car. He stuck his key in the door and turned to me as he opened it. "I'm paying you to find Victoria. And for all I know, she could be dead. And here you are, telling me about a woman you had a fling with." He closed his eyes, shaking his head. "I have nowhere else to turn, Henry. Whoever has her said not to involve the cops. So I'm not willing to take that chance. It's as simple as that. So I'm dependent on you. And—tell me if I'm wrong—I thought you knew what you were doing." He stepped in his car and pulled the door closed behind him without giving me another look.

He started the engine and sat looking at his phone as if I wasn't standing right outside his door.

I turned and walked away. I went back to my car and stepped inside and turned the key in the ignition. As soon as the engine started I remembered something I needed to ask Philip.

I jumped out and left the car running. I ran toward Philip's car. He'd just started to pull from his parking space but stopped. He rolled down the window. "Now what?"

I leaned with one hand on the roof of his car. "This guy Dominic, who works for Charles...I'd like to look into him a little more. He's a big guy. I'd say he's Italian, if I had to guess. Maybe a Long Island guy, the way he talks. But he could be from anywhere up north, really."

Philip shrugged, then shook his head. "I don't know anything about him. Maybe you should talk to—"

There was a loud explosion behind me and sent me face-first into Philip's car. My chin slammed into the top of his door. Glass and debris smashed against the back of my head and covered Philip's car.

I held my arm over my face as I turned to see where the explosion came from.

It was my car.

Flames and black smoke poured from all sides. The hood had been thrown across the parking lot and landed on top of someone else's car.

I ran around to the other side of Philip's car and ducked down behind it. I wasn't sure what would come next.

We looked at each other through the passenger window without saying a word. Even if Philip had spoken, my ears were ringing so loud the only sound I could hear was the ringing mixed with my heart beating inside my head. My ears felt like they were blocked with concrete.

"Get out of here!" I yelled to Philip through the glass. My voice came from my throat as if in slow motion as if I'd yelled into an empty jar.

Philip had no problem with my suggestion. He slammed his car in drive and took off with his tires squealing on the pavement. He drove full speed past the flames pouring from my car. Philip had the Impala up on two wheels as he turned a corner and disappeared down the street.

Chapter 24

AFTER I'D SPENT AT least a solid hour with the officers questioning me as I sat on the back of the EMS vehicle. I looked up as Alex walked toward me.

"Are we done here?" I said as I stood on my own two feet.

"We are," the officer said with a nod.

I gave him a quick nod and walked away with Alex. My ears were still ringing and I strained to hear Alex as we stepped into her Jeep. "I can't hear you," I said, pointing to my ears.

She looked me in the eye and exaggerated the movement of her mouth as she said, "Are...you...sure...you...are...okay?"

I nodded. "My eyes are a little out of whack. It's a little blurry."

Alex kept turning to me as we drove.

"Just watch where you're going," I said. "I'm fine," even though I had a fair amount of pain in the back of my neck from the whiplash and a butterfly stitch on the slice in my chin. "The EMS tech wanted to take me in. Get checked out. Told him you were as smart as any doctor...told him about getting shot, how you fixed me up."

Alex raised her voice more than she normally would driving in the open-topped Jeep. "I'm sure an educated EMS tech appreciates hearing about someone playing doctor with gunshot wounds," she said.

I shrugged. "You do good work, doc."

I looked out to my right as we drove around the San Marco Boulevard rotary. "We need to go see Carla Weiss."

"Again?"

"She might know Dominic."

We were both quiet for a couple of miles until Alex said, "I thought you were being a little paranoid before. About the boat...and getting shot. I'm not sure I can doubt you at this point." She turned to me. "That one was obviously for you."

The ringing in my ears started to ease but my eyes were still blurry with a burning pain. "The question is...is someone trying to stop me from looking for Victoria? Or is there a chance this is Kathleen's husband?"

"I found nothing on her husband. I don't find her anywhere. To be honest. Nothing you told me about her is coming up."

"Maybe I got some things wrong. The time we spent together's a bit foggy. Why do you think I had to detox when I got back?"

We stopped at a red light and Alex turned to me. "Did you know Frank Weiss posted bail last night?"

"He's out?"

She nodded. "I thought maybe you knew."

"No, I was just there yesterday."

• • • • • • • • • •

155

Alex pulled into a space on the street in front of Carla's building.

I sat still for a moment and looked out across the parking lot.

"Are we going in?" Alex said.

"Maybe wait here, see if she comes out? Or...I don't know. I'm afraid if we knock on her door, she'll just do what she did last time."

We sat quiet, watching Carla's building.

"We could be out here all night," Alex said.

She put her hand on my shoulder and when I turned to look at her, Alex nodded toward Carla walking down the stairs toward the parking lot.

I held the binoculars up to my face. Carla had a briefcase in her hand as she stood out in front of her building. A black Lincoln Town Car drove up to the sidewalk and stopped. Carla stepped in through the passenger-side door.

"You see that?" Alex said.

I continued looking through the binoculars, nodding. "Wish I could see the driver." I put the binoculars down as the car pulled away and drove toward the street and turned toward where we were parked. Alex and I slouched in our seats to hide.

The car turned onto 3rd Street.

Alex turned the key and followed behind them.

"Don't get too close," I said as they moved just ahead of us and onto 202.

Alex gave me a look. "You want to drive?"

I kept my mouth shut and let Alex do the driving.

The car with Carla inside turned and headed north on 95. We followed behind as they crossed the Fuller Warren Bridge over the St. Johns and turned onto Park.

Alex said, "Did Philip say what kind of business Carla was involved with?"

"When she was married to Charles, it was the jewelry and gem business. Philip didn't seem to know much about her now."

Alex followed the Lincoln south onto Riverside and until it turned into a parking lot of a very large, expansive Victorian home.

"The Riverdale Inn?" I said as I looked at the wooden sign out front.

Alex parked in the street, which made it hard for us to see past the trees and bushes along the driveway.

"You've never heard of it?" Alex said. "It's a bed and breakfast."

I moved my head, trying to find a better view to see what Carla and whoever was driving the Lincoln were up to.

I sat back in the passenger seat and folded my arms. "What would she be doing here?"

"Afternoon rendezvous?" Alex said.

I shrugged, stood up on the Jeep and put the binoculars up to my eyes. I watched Carla step from the car, walk up the steps and through the front door. She still had the briefcase in her hand.

We both stepped out of the Jeep and moved closer toward the bed and breakfast. We stayed low behind bushes and shrubs, getting as close as we could to get a better view. Alex stopped and crouched down in front of me. She turned and looked at me over her shoulder. "Maybe it's a drug deal?"

"At a bed and breakfast?"

I looked over Alex's shoulder at the Victorian-style home. "Doesn't look to be the place she'd go to buy pot. Although she did say she smoked for medical reasons."

Alex rolled her eyes. "Any adult that smokes will find a reason to say they do it for medical reasons."

I straightened up from behind her. "Wait here. I'll see if I can get a good look at the driver." I walked from one tree to the next, moving toward the front entrance without being noticed.

I stopped and hid behind the trunk of a live oak when I saw two men carry a wooden crate out the front entrance and down the stairs. The Town Car's trunk lid opened and the two carefully slid the crate inside, then closed the trunk.

The driver didn't get out. The two men walked around the side of the building and disappeared. A moment later Carla walked out the door and lit a cigarette as soon as she was outside in the open air. She walked down the steps and got into the Lincoln.

A van drove around the same side of the building where the two men had gone. The van turned right onto Riverside and was gone.

I turned and ran as fast as I could to Alex's Jeep out in the street. Alex was already belted in with the engine running.

"Hurry," she said.

I still had somewhat of a limp but grabbed the roll bar and slid into the passenger seat. Alex hit the gas and we were off. She made a quick u-turn and followed Carla and the Lincoln, heading north on Riverside.

We'd already fallen behind with heavy traffic and six cars between us.

"I'd love to know what's in that crate," I said.

Alex looked straight ahead at the road. "You think it's the sculpture?"

"That would be convenient."

Chapter 25

ALEX AND I SLOUCHED in our seats, staying low, trying to look up over the dashboard from inside the Jeep. We watched the front entrance of the Jacksonville Gem and Mineral Society. The Lincoln was parked in front of the building. But nobody got out.

The front door of the building opened and Julie Sanders—the Society's director—walked down the steps toward the car. She looked back and forth then opened the back passenger door and ducked inside.

A figure stood in the doorway and looked out toward the car.

"Isn't that the old lady?" Alex said.

"Annie?" I nodded. "I think it is."

A moment later Julie stepped out from the car along with the driver. I recognized him right away. "Look who it is," I said to Alex, trying to keep my voice low. "It's Dominic."

"Charles's bodyguard?"

Dominic stepped from the driver's side as the trunk popped open. He walked to the rear of the car, reached inside and removed the wooden crate without anyone else's help. He seemed to struggle somewhat at first. But once he got his footing he carried it up the stairs and into the building. Julie followed him, but Carla didn't get out of the car.

Annie stepped away as Dominic and Julie walked inside. She stuck her head out the door, looked back and forth, and closed the door behind her.

"We could go down, walk right inside and ask what it is," I said.

A moment later, Dominic walked out of the building. He stepped back in the driver's side of the Lincoln and drove away.

"They're coming right this way," I said.

Alex pulled away just as they turned from the driveway. She turned down another side road and waited until they passed.

"Let's go back," I said. "I want to see what's in that crate."

"Right now?"

"We wait and who knows if it'll still be there."

Alex put the Jeep in drive and pulled back out onto the road. "You think Charles has something to do with this?"

"I can't imagine so. Unless they lied about their alleged frigid relationship."

"You mean Charles and Carla?" Alex said.

"No, I'm talking about Julie and Charles. They have no love for each other...it just wouldn't make sense they'd do anything together, even if Carla's playing the middleman."

"Maybe Dominic's two-timing," Alex said. "Goes behind Charles's back with the ex-wife?"

Alex parked the Jeep up on the hill, facing the building.

"We see what's in the crate, we'll know what we're dealing with. If there's no pelican inside, then we assume whatever business they have together has nothing to do with Philip."

I stepped out of the Jeep. "Wait here," I said. "In case some-one else shows up."

Alex unstrapped her seat belt. "I should come with you." She reached under her seat and pulled out her Glock. She tucked it into her waist and followed behind me.

We were careful as we walked down the hill toward the building. We again moved from tree-to-tree and ducked be-hind bushes as we moved closer.

Once we were outside the building I leaned against the ex-terior wall, and peaked inside the window. Julie had a pry bar in her hand as she tried to crack open the top of the crate. She looked inside.

Annie, the old lady, turned toward the window as if she noticed me looking in at them. I ducked out of the way and the light from inside disappeared. She'd closed the blinds.

I walked up the steps of the front door.

In a hushed voice Alex said, "What the hell are you doing?"

I looked at her but didn't answer as I pushed the doorbell.

A moment later the locks clicked and the door opened. It was the old woman, Annie. She stood just inside the doorway and smiled.

"May I help you?" she said.

"Annie, right? Do you remember me? It's Henry. I was here the other day." I tried to look past her. "Is Julie here?"

She smiled as she looked back at me but didn't say a word.

"May I come in?" I said.

Alex stepped up behind me and waved her hand with a smile. "Hi, Annie."

Julie walked up behind the old woman and nudged her aside. She stood in the door but kept it nearly closed behind her. "Sorry, you've come at the wrong time once again. We're not open." She pointed out the door toward a small wooden sign, nailed to the right of the door. "See? Our hours are right there on the sign. You can get them on our website, too." She cleared her throat. "I'm sorry, it's Mr. Walsh, correct?"

I nodded. "Henry. We were just driving by so I thought I'd come say hello."

"Sorry," she said. "We're in the middle of something. The office is closed, although I really wish I could let you in. But, for security reasons..."

"Well, I saw that black Lincoln out front, thought maybe now would be a perfect time to come in."

"I'm actually late for an appointment," Julie said. "We're going to lock up. Maybe you can stop by another time...just take a look at our hours. Again, right there on the sign." She started to close the door but I put my foot up onto the threshold and kept it from closing.

Julie was tall, maybe just an inch or two short of my six-two frame. Being down a step from her meant I had to stretch myself, on my toes, to try and see past her. I caught a glimpse of the crate. "Hey, what's in that crate? I saw you just had it delivered?"

Julie stepped outside and pulled the door closed behind her, but she kept her hand on the knob behind her back. "That's none of your business, Mr. Walsh."

"Please." With a smile, I said, "Call me Henry."

Julie opened the door just enough so she could squeeze back through the doorway. She did what she could to make sure I couldn't see much else. "Have a good night," she said. She closed the door and popped the deadbolt.

Alex and I stood quiet on the steps.

I said, "Could she make it any more obvious she's hiding something?"

The door opened again. Julie stood in the doorway with a phone in her hand. "I'm calling the sheriff's office right now if you don't get off this property."

"You sure you'd want them showing up? Because, I can't help but think the last thing you want is law enforcement seeing what's in that crate."

"You have quite the imagination, Mr. Walsh." She looked back and forth from me to Alex. "Next time I look outside, I hope—for your sake—you're gone."

Chapter 26

I ARRIVED EARLY AT a small café in San Marco, crowded for a weekday afternoon. I sat at a table on the sidewalk patio and ordered a Jack Daniels.

I was onto my second when Kathleen walked up behind me and ran her hand across my back. "Thanks for meeting me, Henry."

I forced a smile—a smirk—as she sat down across from me. She looked as beautiful as ever.

I didn't even wait for her to order a drink. "I'm not into married women," I said. "I follow spouses who cheat for a living. But I'm usually the one on the outside looking in. I'm not interested."

"Henry, please." She paused, her gaze toward the table. "I understand. I do. And I know it doesn't make a difference now, but I told you the truth when I said my husband and I aren't together." She removed her sunglasses, placed them inside her purse.

"Mind if I order a drink?"

I shrugged. "Of course now...go right ahead."

I flagged down the waitress and ordered Kathleen a glass of wine.

I ordered another Jack...and made it a double.

"I don't like looking over my shoulder," I said. "I've had some strange things happen to me lately. And I can't help but wonder if it's got something to do with your husband."

The waitress put a glass of wine down on the table. Kathleen took a sip. Her bright, brown eyes looked at me over the rim. She placed it down and ran her fingers along the stem. "You don't have anything to worry about, Henry."

I leaned back in the chair, my glass in my hand. "Well, now that the cat's out of the bag...why don't you tell me what your husband does for a living?"

"My husband?" She looked down into her glass. "He's an entrepreneur."

"An entrepreneur?"

She nodded. "He's involved in international business. He does a lot of work overseas...export and import."

"Are you trying to avoid telling me what he actually does? Or do you really have no idea?" I leaned forward and took a sip from my glass. "Forgive me for saying this, but you describe his work the way someone married to a mobster might describe her husband's line of work. But normally that'd be waste disposal."

She raised her eyebrows and sipped her wine without responding.

I leaned forward on the table. "Kathleen, I don't even know your last name. How am I supposed to believe anything you say if all you give me are foggy details."

"I told you, Henry. There's nothing to worry about. I just think it's best—for both of us—you let this go. And in time, you'll know more."

"I'm sorry, Kathleen, I—"

She reached across the table and put her hand on top of mine. "Henry, please. Can't we talk about something else?"

I pulled my hand away and looked around at the crowd. "Is it really just a coincidence you showed up when bad things started happening to me? The boat I lived on blew up. My friend's fiancé is missing. And I've been shot..."

Kathleen forced a smile. "You're being paranoid, Henry. I assure you...what happened between us is—" She looked past me and slipped her sunglasses over her eyes. "My husband is not after you. I just hope, one day, maybe you'll give this another chance."

She stood from the table.

I looked up at her. "You're leaving?"

She stepped around the table, leaned down and gave me a kiss. She held her hand against my face for a moment, turned and walked away.

• • • ● • ● • • • •

I made my way inside the restaurant and sat down at the bar. I worried, maybe I'd been too hard on Kathleen. Maybe she was right. Maybe I *was* paranoid...reading too much into everything.

But whether or not I was being paranoid didn't matter. She'd lied to me. More than once. And even if she claimed it was over between her and her husband, she was clearly protecting him by not telling me who he was or what he did for a living.

It did occur to me, however, that she could've been trying to protect me.

I received a text from Alex:

Where are you?

Having a drink

Alone?

Yes

You get a car?

Yes. Billy hooked me up

With what?

Chevy Impala. I'll call you before I leave. I'm going to talk to Frank

Where?

His apartment

You want me to go with you?

I don't know. I'll call you

I stayed at that bar longer than I'd wanted to. And by the time I pulled into the parking lot of Frank's apartment, it was already dark.

I knocked on his door and was caught a little off guard when the door opened right away. Frank stood in the doorway wearing a white tank-top. He held one hand behind his back.

I nodded toward his arm. "You don't need a gun, do you?"

He dropped his hand down by his side with what looked like a .45 in his hand. He narrowed his eyes. "What the hell are you doing here?"

"Is that how you treat all your guests?"

Frank stared back at me but didn't answer.

I said, "I want to ask you some more questions, now that you're free to talk. At least for now."

He shrugged and leaned with his arm up against the frame of the door.

"What can you tell me about Carla Weiss and Julie Sanders?"

He looked out into the hallway. "I'll be right back." He closed the door.

I stood still for a moment and wondered if he'd come back out. I turned and looked down over the railing toward a small pond I hadn't noticed before. The moon reflected off the top of the water.

Frank opened the door wearing a different shirt. He tucked his gun into the front of his pants and walked past me toward the stairs. "We can go sit by the pool."

I was more than surprised Frank was suddenly willing to talk to me. Suspicious might be a better word. On our way down the stairs, I looked out over the parking lot thinking maybe I'd see Alex's Jeep pull in.

Over his shoulder, Frank said, "So, why are you asking about Julie Sanders?"

"I've just gotten to know her. We met a couple of times. The first time she was friendly. The next time, not so much. Maybe because she knew I saw Carla Weiss deliver a crate. She was with someone who works for Charles Weiss."

Frank stopped on the stairs and turned to me. "Charles doesn't have two pennies to rub together, but he's got someone working for him?"

I followed Frank as he turned and walked along a concrete path with lights on the ground along the concrete walkway. He pushed open a metal gate that clanked behind me when I let it close.

Frank pulled the .45 from his waist and placed it on a round plastic table. We sat down across from each other. There was nobody around.

He lifted his leg up almost as high as the table, showed me the bracelet on his ankle. "This is about as far as I can go for now."

I gave a quick nod, but wanted to get right to it. "So, what do you know about Julie Sanders?"

Frank took a moment before he answered. "The Sanders family used to be real wealthy. One of the wealthiest in the area."

"*Used* to be?"

He nodded. "As we both know...nothing lasts forever." He looked up at the apartment buildings surrounding the pool. "You think I ever thought I'd be living like this, in some shitty apartment building, sharing it with some kid half my age?"

I shrugged, looked down toward the blue, sparkling water. "Got a nice pool though."

Frank gave me a look.

"So what is the deal with you and Jayray, anyway?" I said. "I guess I find it a little strange."

"He works for me." Frank pulled a pack of cigarettes from his pants pocket and threw them up on the table. "He's a smart kid, you know. Tells me he was a straight-A student in high school. Sometimes he'll talk about stuff, doesn't even make sense to me. You'd be surprised. He's smarter than he looks."

"So now he gets to learn from you...show him how to steal a pregnant woman's car?"

"I didn't know what you were going to do...figured you were still pissed off about what happened between us the other day."

Frank pulled a couple of mini liquor bottles from his pocket and put them out on the table. He cracked the top open on one and shot it back, straight down his throat. He handed me the other.

I cracked the top and took a sip. Had to choke it down with a taste too close to gasoline. "So...go ahead. About Julie Sanders?"

Frank nodded, pulled a cigarette from his pack. "I'd heard Julie was getting involved in some business deals. I'm sure that's why she took that position, running the Jewel and Gem Society."

"Any chance Carla Weiss'd be working with her?"

Frank narrowed his eyes. "How big was the crate?"

I held my hand out a few feet off the ground and showed him the height. "Four feet high?"

"She delivered it alone?"

I shook my head. "This guy, Dominic. He works for Charles. Drove a black Lincoln...carried the crate inside."

Frank leaned back in his seat and pulled another bottle from his pocket. He cracked the top and tipped his head back to finish it off. "You know, Julie used to be tied-in real tight with the international trade market. She knows the same people Charles knows, over there in France."

"She didn't have anything good to say about Charles. She said they threw him out, took away his membership for trying to scam another member."

Frank took a drag of his cigarette. "I don't know much about whatever it is you heard. But Charles knows a lot of people.

If there's any friction between those two—I'd have to put my money on Charles."

"Charles thinks Julie set him up to keep him away."

Frank shook his head. "This business..." He had his chair turned out from the table, facing the pool. He leaned back and crossed one leg over the other, his hand with the cigarette rested on his knee. He looked toward the ground. "I'm trying to be fair with you, Henry. Telling you whatever you ask. Don't you think it'd make sense you do the same?"

"How so?"

He looked me right in the eye and waited a moment before he spoke. "Tell me where my brother is."

I reached across the table and grabbed another snifter, cracked the top and shot the gasoline-like liquor down the back of my throat.

"If I knew he were alive, I'd tell you. And if I find out where he is—if it turns out he's alive—you'll be the first to know."

Frank sat quiet for a moment, taking a drag of his cigarette. "You don't know what was in that crate?"

"Are you asking me because you wonder if it's the crystal pelican you're all after?"

Frank shrugged his shoulders and leaned forward, his elbows on his knees. "If Philip's alive, and if he's hiding, maybe he worked out a deal with someone like Julie. But I don't know why Carla'd be involved. I can't say for sure Charles and Carla are even on speaking terms." Frank had one eye closed as he took a drag from his cigarette. The smoke floated toward his face. "Maybe Julie and Carla teamed-up?"

"What about the tough guy working for Charles?"

Frank stared out toward the pool. "Philip and Carla have some history, you know."

"Really? Philip and Carla?"

Frank nodded.

"Then, how would Julie fit in?" I said.

"I don't know," Frank said. "Maybe she lined-up a buyer. They cut Charles out of the deal, Jeanpaul gets his money."

"Jeanpaul? He's the artist?"

"Yeah. That's one thing about Philip, he believes the artist should always be taken care of." Frank shrugged again. "I'm just making guesses. Isn't that how it works?"

I said, "How *what* works?"

"As a private investigator, no? I'm saying, don't you just make an educated guess? Solve the mystery?"

"Not quite," I said. Although he wasn't that far off from the truth. "What about you? You must not be happy, Philip cut you out of the deal after you and Charles had worked something out?"

Frank gave me a look and held his stare for a moment. He reached for his .45 and pulled it closer to his side of the table. "You asking me if I'd kill my own brother?"

"Well, you're the one who insists he's alive. I can't help but think maybe you know a little something about what went down that day in the marina."

Frank stood up from the table, picked up his gun and let it hang down by his side. He dropped his cigarette on the ground, stomped it out with his foot and kicked it into the pool. He walked away without saying another word, opened the gate and let it slam behind him with a loud bang.

Chapter 27

IT WAS EARLY MORNING when I pulled into the parking lot of Carla's apartment building. The sun was still making its way over the horizon. The only sounds came from the laughing gulls and the waves crashing out at the beach behind her building.

I looked at my watch and wondered if it was too early. I made my way up the stairs anyway and knocked on her door. I looked forward to her surprise.

But I was the one surprised when she pulled open the door as soon as I'd knocked. Like she was expecting me. She stood in front of me in a bikini and the same kimono she wore the first time I met her. She held a bath towel in her hand as she wiped down her wet hair.

"Early bird gets the worm," she said as she turned from the door, leaving it wide open for me to go in. "Just put on some coffee, if you'd like a cup."

I didn't have a chance to answer before she poured me a cup and handed it to me. "Sorry, I don't drink milk."

I took a sip and nodded. "Black's good."

She said, "It's nice to see an attractive man at my door first thing in the morning." She winked, then grabbed her cup from the table and walked out into the living room area. She reached down and pointed the remote at the TV. She turned up the volume on a Steely Dan song I didn't know the name of but had heard a hundred times before.

"So what do I owe this visit?" She reached into a glass ashtray and picked up what was left of a joint. She lit it, took a hit, and held it out toward me.

I hesitated, but waved her off, "No, not today." I followed her out onto the patio.

With her back to me, she leaned out over the railing looking toward Neptune Beach.

"Must pay quite a bit for a place like this, overlooking the beach," I said.

She turned to me and shrugged a shoulder without answering as she took another hit from the joint.

"I've been looking for a place myself. Not sure I could afford something like this. But since somebody blew up the boat I was living on..." I let that hang for a moment.

She played it cool. "Maybe I could use a roommate." Carla raised her cup of coffee to her mouth and gave me a look over the top as she took a sip.

"Actually, I was curious how one might afford a place like this. Oceanview...the beach right there beyond the palm trees. I mean, I don't make a lot of money. I don't know what you do for a living, but..." I took a sip of coffee. "Did you say you were in the art business? Maybe something has to do with jewels and gems?"

Carla's eyelids hung down over her eyes, the weed hitting home. "I don't remember talking about what I do for a living. I guess you could say I freelance."

"Freelance?"

She nodded as she sat down in a white, wicker chair facing the ocean. "I do whatever I need to do to pay my rent. Sometimes I help broker deals, sometimes I—"

"You do deliveries?"

Carla gave me a curious look. "Deliveries?"

"We don't have to play games here, Carla."

"What kind of games?" She had a crooked smile on her face but seemed to want to hold it back. Maybe it was the pot.

"I know you delivered a crate to Julie Sanders. I saw you."

The smile dropped from her face. She looked down into her coffee, put the cup down next to her and got up from her chair. She stood next to me and leaned with her elbows on the top of the railing.

I put my cup down and folded my arms at my chest as I leaned next to her.

She turned to me and shrugged. "Just a little side gig," she said.

"Are you working with Charles?"

"Charles?" She shook her head. "Not a chance."

"Julie Sanders?"

She looked out toward the water. "I've known Julie for a long time. We help each other out once in a while. There's not much else to it."

"And what about Dominic? I saw him behind the wheel...carrying that big crate inside."

176

Carla rubbed her temples. "I have a migraine. That's why I smoke."

"The pot?"

She nodded. "It helps."

"Didn't you just take a couple hits?"

She turned and sat down in the chair and leaned her head back with her eyes closed.

"Why don't you just tell me what was in that crate?" I said.

Carla got up from her chair again and walked back into the apartment. She came back out a moment later with a cigarette in her hand, cupped her hand around a lighter and lit her smoke. "I don't know what was in it. I delivered it. I collected some money. That's all I was supposed to do."

"You didn't ask?"

She shrugged as she shook her head.

"You still haven't said what Dominic was doing there. Is he someone you hired? Or is he more than just Charles's bodyguard."

"I went out to see Charles last week, told him I needed some muscle. He said, 'Don't look at me' but then Dominic came into the room—must've overheard us—said he'd help."

"Did Charles know you were working with Julie?"

Carla shook her head. "Are you kidding? Charles and Julie?" She took a drag from her cigarette then exhaled with her head tilted back. She blew the smoke straight up into the air.

She was quiet, looking at me. "When I saw you at my door, I'd hoped you were here for more of a *social* visit." She got up and walked back inside.

As I followed her in she put her cigarette down in the glass ashtray on the half-wall that divided the kitchen from the rest of the apartment.

She turned and said, "So since this clearly isn't a social stop...then what is it you want from me?"

"First of all, Philip's fiancé is missing. I need to find her. But I'm pretty sure—if I have it right—whoever's after the crystal pelican is responsible for kidnapping Victoria and blowing up Philip's boat."

She turned and reached toward the ashtray, picked up her cigarette and took another drag. "Where is Philip now? I thought he was dead?"

"I don't know. He might be. But that doesn't mean I'll stop looking for Victoria."

She took another drag and nodded. "I don't know who she is—we've never met—but I know she comes from a lot of money. Just like Philip, they were both born with silver spoons in their mouths."

I thought about what she'd said, through words of apparent bitterness.

"I just hope you're being honest with me. I was there the morning Victoria went missing. And I promised Philip I'd look for her, no matter what. If you're lying about any of this..."

She smiled as she took another drag from her cigarette, a devious look in her eyes. She shrugged. "Why would I lie?"

Chapter 28

BILLY WAS BEHIND THE bar when I sat down across from him. He wiped down the space in front of me and gave me a nod with his chin. "Where've you been?" he said. "Thought I'd at least see you down here for a drink at some point."

"Sorry, honey," I said. "Truth is, I'm thinking of cutting back a bit."

"Yeah?"

I shrugged. "Can't help thinking...if I hadn't had a couple of bourbons at Skip's maybe I would've avoided that bullet. Not to mention, I don't think my body handles the next day the way it used to."

Billy nodded slowly. "So what's that mean, you're on the wagon?"

I shook my head. "Like I said, I'm just thinking about it."

He leaned with his hands on the bar, his arms out wide. He hung his head and looked back and forth along the bar. "Personally, I found drinking a hell of a lot more enjoyable when I was younger. And you're right, the hangovers hang longer with age. Truth is, the fastest way for a guy in my position to go under is to over-consume his own product." Billy sipped from a cup. "Have I ever told you about a friend of mine who used to own Jimmy's Pizza?"

I shook my head.

"He always liked a drink here and there. But when he expanded the place and opened up a bar next door." Billy made a motion with his hand, fingers out straight, moved it like a rollercoaster heading down. "After a while, he sat at his own bar—day and night— and drank away his profits. He'd get drunk and offer to buy anyone who walked in the door a drink."

"Let me guess...he went out of business?"

Billy shook his head. "Walked in the front door of his house one night—after half a bottle of whiskey, from what I hear—tripped over the threshold and cracked his head on the floor."

I looked at Billy. "What happened?"

Billy shrugged. "He died."

I stared back at Billy for a moment. "Couldn't that've happened to him sober?"

Billy nodded. "Sure. But I'm just saying..."

I gave Billy a look. "I'll have an iced tea."

I looked down at my watch, then glanced back toward the door. I said to Billy, "So I'm thinking maybe I should get a place out toward the beach."

"Upstairs not doing it for you?"

"Oh, no. It's great. I mean, I appreciate you giving me a place to sleep...and the office space. It's just, I don't know. I was over at this place out at Neptune Beach and—"

"Neptune Beach? Where you were shot?"

I nodded and sipped my iced tea.

Billy put his finger up in the air and stepped over toward the beer tap and filled a couple of pints. He carried them over to two women seated a few stools away. He came back and stood in front of me as he wiped his hands with a towel. "Sorry, go ahead."

"Don't get me wrong," I said. "I loved living on the river. But there's something about the ocean. I don't know, maybe I'd rent an apartment or one of those small cabins just off the beach." I turned when the door opened behind me, expecting to see Alex. But it was Earl, one of Billy's old-time regulars.

I looked down at my watch again and said to Billy, "Alex was supposed to be here by now."

Earl walked by and raised his hand toward me with a quick wave. "Hey, Henry."

Billy poured a drink for Earl and put it down on the bar where he always sat.

My phone rang. I answered, "Henry Walsh."

"Henry? It's Carla. I need your help. Please."

"Where are you?" I looked up at Billy watching me.

"Is it Alex?" he said.

I shook my head at him.

Carla said, "I need you to come over right away."

I thought for a moment, not sure if she was in trouble or if she was trying to seduce me. "I'm in the middle of something," I said. "Can you tell me what...Carla?"

I looked at my phone. The call'd been disconnected.

I tossed a couple of bills on the bar. "I gotta go," I said. "Do me a favor...if Alex shows up, have her call me."

"Did you try calling her?"

I nodded. "She didn't answer."

• • • ● • ● • • ·

The Chevy Impala I was driving came cheap. I'd bought it from Billy's cousin, who admitted it might've had some problems, and warned me not to take it too far until I had it looked at by a mechanic.

But 'too far' was relative.

I took the ramp from 295 and headed east on 10. I tried calling Carla's phone but she didn't answer. The call went right to voicemail. It was one of the generic messages: The wireless caller you're trying to reach is not available.

I wondered what I'd be walking into at Carla's. The idea of her seducing me wasn't a horrible thought, although I didn't really expect that's why she'd called. I wondered if she was in danger...

And that's when the Impala's engine started to stink with a burning odor...the smell of rotten eggs. Then I smelled burning rubber. "Not now," I said. The engine made a sputtering sound, like I was about to run out of gas. But I had a full tank.

The engine stalled. I put the pedal to the floor as I turned the key in the ignition as I coasted into the next lane. The engine wouldn't turn over. I leaned hard into the steering wheel, with the power steering no longer working; turning the wheel was almost impossible.

Horns were blowing all around me...cars whizzing by.

I thought about the car and what my father said the first time I bought a Plymouth Scamp for two hundred dollars. "You get what you pay for."

I didn't know where Alex was. Carla was possibly in danger. And here I was, sitting in the breakdown lane in a broken down Chevy Impala I hadn't even owned for three days.

Chapter 29

BILLY SHOWED UP AN hour after I called him. The tow truck had already left with my car hooked up on the back. The driver offered me a ride, but couldn't take me out to Neptune Beach.

We drove in Billy's smooth, new Lexus with plush leather seats. "Raz was at Alex's house, on the couch," he said. "Not Alex, though. She wasn't there. And her Jeep was gone."

"She's not answering her calls," I said as Billy turned into the parking lot. He parked in front of Carla's apartment complex.

I opened the door to step out and turned to him. "You want to wait here while I go see what's up?"

He shook his head and stepped out from the Lexus.

We walked toward the building and up the stairs. We stepped off onto Carla's floor and turned the corner toward her apartment. Her door was cracked open.

Billy sniffed and whispered under his breath, "I smell weed."

I pushed on the door and walked in ahead of Billy. Carla was on the couch. But she wasn't alone.

Frank and Jayray stood across from her, the coffee table between them. All three turned and looked toward me and Billy. Frank with a gun in his hand, he turned and pointed it toward us. He waved the muzzle of the gun upward, gesturing for us to put our hands up. "Get 'em up," he said.

I looked from Carla to Frank. "What a surprise," I said. "Mind telling me what the hell this is all about?"

He waved the gun toward the couch. "You know what it's all about. Go ahead and sit your ass down. Both of you. No-body'll need to get hurt if you behave yourself."

Billy and I moved toward Carla and sat on either side of her.

"Where's Alex?" I said, looking at Frank.

"Who the hell's Alex?" he said.

"Don't play dumb with me. Where is she?"

He laughed. "Throwing demands around like that...but I'm the one with the gun?"

I looked down at his ankle, the bracelet they put on him no longer there. "Don't you think the cops will come looking for you?"

Frank looked at Jayray and gave him a quick nod with his chin. Jayray stepped toward me and knocked what looked like a Saturday Night Special against the side of my head. I turned my face just as he stepped toward me and somewhat softened the blow.

I felt the warmth of my own blood running down my face. "Was that really necessary?"

Frank said, "I told him you do a lot of talking, do what he needs to shut you up."

I turned and looked at Carla. Her eyes were red. More than normal. It was hard to tell if it'd been from crying or the smell of weed in the air.

"Carla here refused to tell me where the pelican is. And I'm having a hard time believing anything that comes out of her mouth."

Carla said, "I told you already, I don't know where it—"

Frank pointed his gun at Carla and put his other hand up to his mouth, holding his finger in front of his lips. "Shhhh." He slowly shook his head. "Remember what I said? Only speak when spoken to." Frank turned to me. He shifted the gun my way. "Are you ready to tell me where Philip is? I'm sick of playing games."

"I already told you I don't know if he's even alive."

"Yeah?" said Frank, his thick eyebrows up high on his head. "Is that right? What if I told you I know he's alive. And I know he's hiding the pelican? He thinks he can hide in that piece of shit he's been driving? You know he showed up at my door, dressed up in a costume. Like Jayray didn't know it was him."

"If you've seen him, then why the hell are you asking me where he is?"

"Did I say I saw him? I haven't. Not personally, anyway." Frank pointed the gun back at Carla. "Who'd you meet at the bed and breakfast? Was it Philip?"

I gave Billy a quick look. He seemed calm, not saying a word. But I could tell by looking at him his wheels were turning, the way he shifted his gaze all around the room.

Carla said to Frank, "Riverdale Inn. I didn't meet anybody, I was paid to pick up a box—a crate—and deliver it. It was there waiting for me. It's just some jewels."

Frank shook his head. "You believe this bullshit?"

186

I looked over at Jayray, sweat coming down the side of his face. He was quiet, a bit lazy with his gun hanging down by his side.

Out of the corner of my eye I watched Billy shift himself forward toward the front of the couch cushion. He gave me a quick glance without turning his head.

There was a cup of what looked like black coffee on the coffee table next to a tall vase filled with cut flowers in water.

Frank held up his .45. "You keep playing dumb with me, Carla, and I'm going to have to use this. To be honest, I'd hate to have to mess up such a pretty face. But I've had enough."

"I'm telling you the truth," she said. "That crate was waiting for me. We picked it up and delivered it. That's all there was to it."

For the first time since we walked in the door, Billy opened his mouth. He nodded toward the corner. "Is this crystal sculpture I keep hearing about—does it look anything like that?" He looked toward the space behind Frank and Jayray.

They both turned at the same time.

Billy got his foot up on the edge of the coffee table and grabbed the vase as he propelled himself toward Frank. He had the vase up in the air and smashed it on the top of Frank's head.

Frank's eyes went white and rolled up into his skull. He stumbled backwards and crashed on top of the television behind him.

I grabbed the cup of coffee and threw it at Jayray's face. The coffee splashed all over him as he ducked but the cup bounced off his head. I stepped over the table and knocked the gun from his hand.

His Saturday Night Special slid under a chair behind him. But instead of reaching for it he ran for the door. I dove and wrapped my arms around his feet and took him down hard to the floor. His head bounced off the flowered linoleum in the kitchen.

Jayray tried to break free from my hold. He kicked his feet. But I squeezed tighter. I wouldn't let go of his legs. He reached for the cup on the floor and threw it behind him, trying to hit me. As I put my hand up to knock it away I had to let go of his legs. He kicked me under the chin and broke free, up on his feet and out the door.

I turned and saw Billy standing over Frank.

Frank didn't move. He had blood coming down his face, then moaned as he opened his eyes and looked toward Carla.

Out of the corner of my eye I caught the Saturday Night Special pointed right at me. I turned and looked at Carla, her arms extended, her finger on the trigger.

Chapter 30

CARLA PICKED FRANK'S .45 off the floor and held it toward us. She placed the Saturday Night Special in her purse. "The three of you," she said. "Get out on the balcony."

Billy and I looked at each other.

"Carla, what the hell are you doing?" I said.

"Just get out there. I don't have time for this." She waved the gun toward the balcony. "Let's go."

Billy and I walked through the sliding glass doors onto the balcony. Frank was just starting to come to, and stumbled out behind us. The lock clicked from the inside and Carla walked backwards away from us, the gun still in her hand. She disappeared out the front door.

Frank groaned. Billy pulled a towel off the porch railing and tossed it at him. Frank held it up to his face.

I looked down at the wicker chair, picked it up and tossed it at the glass. It bounded off the glass without making a single crack. I tried again, this time lifting the chair high up over my head. I threw it down as hard as I could into the glass doors.

The door shattered. Pieces of glass covered the floor of the balcony and inside Carla's apartment.

I carefully stepped through the opening, trying not to step on any glass. Billy followed right behind me. "She's got to be long gone by now," I said. I looked back at Frank, still outside leaning against the railing. "You'd better put some ice on that."

I peeked into a bedroom where the bed had nothing more than a mattress on top. There was a dresser with drawers open and empty, and a closet with nothing inside but a handful of hangers on the rod.

"She's not coming back," I said.

Frank walked past the bedroom toward the kitchen. He opened the freezer door. I heard him say, "No shit, genius." Frank took ice from the freezer and put it inside the towel he held in his hand. "Where the hell'd Jayray go?"

Billy and I headed for the door. I turned in the doorway and looked back at Frank. "He ran. You missed him. That's what you get for taking a nap."

Frank put his hand on his head, looked at the blood on his fingers. "Jesus Christ, look what you did. I'm going to need stitches. How the hell am I supposed to pay for that? I don't have insurance."

Billy, standing out in the hallway now, gave Frank a nod. "I'll cover it for you."

Billy was tough when he had to be; generous as anyone when he wanted to be. His father taught him how to protect himself. His mother taught him to cook and take care of people.

And I knew he didn't take any pleasure cracking Frank in the head, but he knew the alternative was one of us'd take a bullet.

"Help me find that pelican," I said. "Nobody'll have to worry about a thing."

Frank walked out the door past us and headed down the stairs with the towel and ice on his head. "I was about to find out, until you showed up."

"Carla?" I said.

Frank gave a slight nod. "That's what I was gettin' at."

The three of us got to the bottom of the stairs.

Frank lit a cigarette. "That piece of shit." His back to me, he said to himself, "Friggin' kid took the car."

I nodded with my chin toward the street. "Looks like there's a bus stop over there," I said.

"You can't give me a ride?" Frank said.

Billy had already walked away, headed toward his Lexus.

I turned to Frank. "You held a gun on us. Now you're asking for a ride?"

"I thought you were working with Carla. She told me you were helping her. That's why she called you."

I shook my head. "Not a chance." I walked toward the Lexus, Billy waiting inside with the engine running.

Frank followed behind me. Come on, Henry. Just drop me off at—"

"Call Jayray," I said. "I'm sure he'll come pick you up."

I heard Frank say, "Shit, my phone. What'd I do with my phone?"

· · ● ● · ● ● · ·

My phone rang again. I didn't recognize the number. "Walsh Investigations," I said.

"Henry, it's Philip."

"Philip? Where the hell are you?"

191

"It doesn't matter. Listen to me. I found Victoria."

It took a moment to register. "Victoria? Found her where? Is she okay?"

"I don't know. I hope so. She's in Sydney."

"I don't understand. How could she be—"

"She said she'd explain everything when I got out there...told me to fly out as soon as I could."

"Are you sure? You need to be careful before you just get on a plane and—"

"Don't worry, Henry," he said. "I just need to get down there."

We were both quiet for a moment.

"You there?" I said.

"Henry, I need you to do something for me."

"If it's to look for someone ten thousand miles away...I'm not sure."

"I might've found the crystal pelican. But you'll need to help us get it."

"Us?"

"Don't worry about the details," Philip said. "I'll be in touch."

"Philip, none of this makes sense. You're not telling me everything. I'm starting to wonder if I'm caught up in some game. Don't take this the wrong way, but I'm starting to wonder if you blew up your own boat."

Philip was quiet for a moment. "Henry?" He paused. "Why would I do that?"

"Did you?"

"I have to go, we're boarding now."

I looked down at my phone. Philip hung up.

• • • ●•• ● •• •

It was late when we got to Billy's restaurant and I was relieved to see Alex's Jeep in the parking lot. Billy and I went upstairs, and I couldn't have been happier to see Alex sitting at her desk. "Where've you been?" I said. "I called you…I don't know how many times. Billy went to your house and…"

"Sorry, I left my phone up here on the desk."

"You're kidding? But you were supposed to meet me here."

"I'm sorry. Really. I'll explain later." She looked at my face. "What happened?"

I shook my head and didn't answer her. "Victoria's alive. She called Philip and said she's in Australia."

"Is he sure?"

I shook my head. "I don't know." I thought for a moment. "He also said he has the crystal pelican. Or at least knows where it is…he wants me to help him get it."

Billy turned around an old, wooden chair and sat on it backwards. He leaned forward against the backrest. "Can one of you explain to me the story behind this crystal sculpture everyone seems to be after?"

"It's a big, handmade sculpture of a pelican. It's made of a rare crystal, and I guess they're not normally this large. It was designed by an artist in France, Jeanpaul DePierre. From what I understand, Charles Weiss partnered with the artist. He brought Philip's father in on the deal—I guess to finance the purchase. Charles was the middleman…the broker. But then Philip's father died. They were right in the middle of the deal and it fell apart. According to Charles, Philip's father already

193

had the piece in his possession. I'm not sure that's true. But whoever wants this piece bad enough knows it goes through Philip. It's assumed if he doesn't have it himself, then he knows where it is."

"Did Philip tell you he had it?"

"No, Philip said Frank got involved. And as you can see from what happened earlier…when Frank gets involved in something, chances are good it'll go wrong."

"Seems like a real moron," Billy said.

Alex said, "Charles claims the artist is threatening him. Said he's scared for his life."

I stood at the window overlooking the parking lot, staring into the darkness over the St. Johns. My back was to Billy and Alex. I said, "I don't know who to believe." I turned from the window. "Even Philip. One minute he's begging me to find his fiancé. Next thing he's on a plane heading to Sydney. Now I'm afraid he'd planned his death all along, until I showed up. He of course wasn't expecting me to be there."

"What about your friend, Kathleen?" Billy said. "You still think any of what's happened to you has to do with her?"

I shook my head. "I don't think so."

I looked over at Alex, but she looked away when we caught each other's eyes. I said to her, "Alex, have you heard anything from Mike?"

She shook her head. "No, nothing. But I think maybe it's time you talk to him."

I stared back at Alex without saying a word for a moment. I could feel Billy watching me.

"She's right," Billy said. "Maybe you two should try and work together."

I let out a slight laugh. "Why, because I'm not getting anywhere on my own?"

Alex said, "He's not getting anywhere either. And let's be honest. Whatever—or whoever—we're dealing with here isn't messing around."

"You want Stone to protect me?"

Alex rolled her eyes. "Bombs, bullets, and married women. Not a safe way of life," she said.

Billy got up from his chair and headed for the door. "I gotta get downstairs, see what I've missed, not that I didn't enjoy a little action." He rolled his eyes. "I'll let you two talk this out." He opened the door and disappeared down the stairs.

I turned to Alex. "I didn't know she was married. How many times do I have to tell you that."

"Would it've mattered?"

I paused for a moment. "You really have to ask?"

Alex's phone rang. "It's Mike Stone." She answered the call.

I watched her face, listening carefully. All she said was, "Where?" then waited a moment. "You sure?" She looked over at me, her eyebrows down tight over her eyes. She shook her head, slowly.

I kept watching her. And waited.

She hung up, let her phone hang down in her hand by her side with a frown on her face. I knew whatever Mike had just told her wasn't good news. She started to speak, her mouth slightly open...took a deep swallow and said, "It's Philip. They found him in his car at the airport." She stepped toward me and reached for my hand. "Philip's dead."

Chapter 31

ALEX AND I WAITED in an empty room at the Jacksonville Sheriff's Office with nothing more than a wood-grained folding table and four folding chairs. Alex had persuaded me to meet with Mike Stone.

I agreed to tell him most of what I'd known. Not everything, of course.

I felt an obligation to Philip. I couldn't at the time say for sure what kind of friend he was. Or if we were ever really friends at all.

At the very least, we'd helped each other out over the years. He gave me a boat to live on. Whenever I happened to travel—which wasn't often—he'd be the one to hook me up with a place to stay. That included my time in Ocracoke, where I spent a couple of nights with Kathleen at one of Philip's many vacation homes around the world.

Seated across from me and Alex on the other side of the table, Mike Stone leaned on his elbows with his hands cupped together in front of him. "We're certainly widening the investigation with the information you've provided," he said. "That includes looking for what is apparently stolen property from..." he looked down at the yellow pad in front of him, "Jeanpaul DePierre." He looked up at me. "We now have a homicide case—your friend Philip—in addition to the young woman at Darcy Car Rental. We're also looking at a kidnapping." Mike gave me a look. "I'm doing all I can to hold off charges that could still come your way. I'll do what I can, but you held back information from an investigation. I can't make you any promises. But I'll do my best."

"I'm here now," I said. "And just to be clear...it was all done to protect Philip's fiancé. That's all there was to it."

Mike kept his stare on me for a moment. "Here's the thing, I'm going to have to ask you to back off of whatever it is you're doing...however you're involved in everything." He turned to Alex. "It's for his own good."

"What if I say no?" I said.

His eyebrows both bounced up high on his head. "No?"

I nodded. "That's right. I'm a licensed private investigator. I'm not getting in the way of your investigation. The only difference is I don't move at a snail's pace to get things done."

Detective Stone narrowed his eyes, stared straight at me. "You listen here, Walsh—"

Alex stood from her seat. "He gets it, Mike. We both do." She grabbed me by the arm and pulled me up from the table. "Are we done?" she said.

He nodded and stood up from the table. He walked toward the door and pulled it open. "If I have to ask you again to back off, I can't promise how any of this'll turn out for you." Mike held the door and gestured for us to walk out ahead of him.

· · · · ● ● ● ● · ·

197

As soon as we were outside I said to Alex, "I'm going back out to see Charles Weiss. If you want to come—"

Alex grabbed me by the arm. "Henry, Mike's not kidding. He'll arrest you for getting in the way. Let them handle it. Okay?"

I laughed, and continued toward her Jeep. "He told me to stay out of his way. So that's what I'll do. I'll stay out of his way. But he can't arrest me for doing my job as a private investigator hired by one of the victim's." I walked ahead of her and over my shoulder, said, "You really think he expects me to act like nothing's happened? Go sit on my couch with a bag of chips...wait for him to call me, tell me everything's been taken care of."

I stepped up into Alex's Jeep and gripped the roll bar above my head. She turned hard out of the parking lot, not sure if she was annoyed with me or just in a hurry.

"Listen," I said. "You don't have to be involved. I'll take it from here. That way you're in the clear."

"What happened to fifty-fifty?" she said, giving me a look.

I smiled. "Alex, I know you think we might be a little in over our heads, but—"

She turned to me, her hair blowing in the wind swirling inside the Jeep. "I'll go with you."

"To see Charles?"

With her chin she nodded toward the glovebox. She handed me a separate key. "Open the glove box. Grab the Glock."

• • • ● • ● • • •

We stood at the locked glass door. The blinds were closed and it was almost impossible to see inside. I leaned my face against the tinted window on the front of Charles's office or whatever it was he actually did there.

I could see a figure inside, beyond the front display counter, through the doorway at the back of the store. The only lights on were the ones behind the curtained doorway.

Alex rang the bell next to the sign that read By Appointment Only.

With my face up against the window, I saw the figure turn toward me. It didn't take me more than a split second to realize whoever it was had pointed a gun toward me.

Alex stood in front of the glass door and I jumped into her with my arms extended, throwing her out of the way, down toward the ground.

Loud pops came from the gun inside. The glass on the front door exploded and glass covered our backs. We both jumped to our feet and ran around the side of the brick building. I looked around the corner and a car nearly identical to the one being driven when I was shot was speeding toward us. The tires squealed.

Alex and I ran toward the front of the building as more shots were fired, this time coming from the black Town Car.

We ran through the door where the glass had been blown out and into Charles's shop. We ducked behind the counter and watched the Town Car drive fast right past the entrance. More shots were fired from the vehicle toward Alex's Jeep.

The car's tires squealed. It nearly tipped onto two wheels as it pulled away and left the parking lot.

I helped Alex to her feet and looked her over to make sure she wasn't hit. "You okay?"

She glanced at my arm and I looked at my leg, seeing the blood drip down to the floor. I lifted my elbow and saw the gash, but was sure it wasn't from the bullets. "Just a scratch," I said. I reached my fingers to the wound and realized I had a piece of glass in my arm. I closed my eyes, clenched my teeth, and ripped it free.

"Jesus," Alex said as she turned to look away.

I pushed open the curtains on the doorway and walked into the back area of Charles's shop.

Charles was down on the ground, his mouth covered in duct tape and his hands and legs tied with rope.

I reached down and ripped the tape from his face.

"Ouch!" he said. "Be careful, will you?"

I looked at Alex, and for a second it crossed my mind to put the tape back on Charles's face. But instead I pulled out my knife and cut the rope from his hands and ankles.

"What were they after?" I said as I helped him to his feet.

Charles looked back and forth from Alex to me. "They were going to kill me."

"Who?"

He rubbed his wrists. "I don't know. They wanted me to tell them who had the crystal pelican."

"Do you know?" I said.

He stared back at me. "Do I know *what*? Where the pelican is?"

I nodded.

Charles said, "I wish I did, but..."

"I'm guessing these might be the same people who—" I had to think for a moment. "You probably don't know, but—"

"Know what?"

"About Philip." I glanced back at Alex, leaning behind the doorway with her Glock drawn, keeping an eye out toward the front of the shop. I looked Charles in the eye. "Philip was found dead in his car at the airport."

Charles kept his eyes wide open, his eyebrows high on his balding head. "At the airport? Not from the explosion?"

I shook my head. "Somebody shot him."

Charles had a blank stare to his face. He looked toward the open door off the back of the building.

Alex said, "You have no idea who they were?"

Charles shook his head. "Never seen them before in my life."

I looked around the back room. "Where's your body-guard?"

"Dominic?"

"Yeah. Have you seen him today?"

"He's up in New York. Had some business to take care of."

I felt Alex watching me. I said, "Somewhat of a coincidence, isn't it?"

"You mean, that he's not here when I need him?"

I didn't have to answer. Charles knew that's exactly what I meant. But I also knew there was more to it.

"We saw Dominic driving a car with your ex."

"Carla?"

"Yeah. They delivered a crate together. Picked it up from the Riverdale Inn—"

"Out in Riverside?"

I nodded. "Took it out to the Gem and Mineral Society and delivered it to Julie Sanders." I looked across the room at a workbench built into the wall. There was a briefcase on top that caught my eye. "I'll be honest, Charles, I was almost certain you were involved."

"Carla and I?" Charles shook his head. "We hardly talk."

"She said you're the one...asked Dominic to help her."

"Me? No, why would I?"

I gave Charles a look. "Forgive me for not believing you, but the truth's been hard to come by lately."

"I swear, whatever Carla's got going on has nothing to do with me." Charles opened up a folding chair he had leaning against the wall and sat down, still rubbing his wrists. "I don't understand why Dominic would be helping Carla. I don't think I've ever mentioned her to him...not sure how he'd even know who she is."

"Like I said, she said you had him help her, that she asked you for some muscle."

Charles looked around the room, walked toward a table and reached underneath, came out with a cell phone in his hand. He tapped the screen and put it up against his ear. "I'll find out right now."

"Who are you calling?"

"Dominic."

"No! Hang up," I said.

"Huh? Why? I'll just..."

"Hang up the phone, Charles. Right now."

Charles tapped the screen and put the phone back down on the table.

I said, "Dominic knows I followed them. I already confronted Carla. I'm sure—especially if they're up to something together—she's already told him to watch out for me."

"You think he's behind this? Those men came in here...trying to get me to talk? Dominic's behind it?"

"I can't say for sure, but it looks that way, doesn't it?" I watched Charles, rubbing the top of his bald head. I said, "You don't know a thing about him, do you."

Charles shrugged. "I needed a bodyguard. It's not like I asked for a resume."

Chapter 32

WE WERE IN ALEX'S Jeep on our way out to Darcy Car Rental. Alex had just gotten off the phone with Detective Stone, hoping he'd share any news he had about Philip's death, or if there were any leads.

"Did he agree it sounded like Philip was set up?" I said, looking at Alex from the passenger seat.

"Set up by who?"

"I don't know. But none of this makes sense. One minute, Victoria's making a call to Philip, tells him she's been abducted, next she's down in Sydney?" I looked out the passenger side. "I should've done more to protect him."

"Protect him? You had no idea where he was."

"But someone else obviously did."

Alex gave me a quick glance. "Frank?"

"Philip might've reached out to him. Frank must've told someone where to find Philip."

Alex said, "You're not eliminating Charles from any of this, are you? I have a hard time believing he's as innocent as he'd like us to think." She turned the Jeep into a parking space in front of Darcy Car Rental as a young man walked into the building

He looked up from behind the counter when we walked in. "Welcome to Darcy Car Rental," he said. His hair slicked back with a glowing shine. He wore a tie and a sports coat, but he had a baby face, like he'd yet to have to shave. He seemed proud to be dressed up like a big boy, his sleeves a few inches long for his short arms. "How can I help you today?" he said.

I looked at his name tag. "Tyler," I said.

He followed my eyes and also looked at the tag pinned to his sports coat. With a nod he said, "Yes, sir."

"I'm hoping you can help me out. I don't know how long you've been here, but I know about a tragedy you all experienced right in this building, not too long ago."

His smile was gone from his face. He nodded. "I've been here for a few months. I was working here when it happened."

"You were here?"

He shook his head. "Not the same day. I just meant..."

"That's not actually why I'm here." I pulled a piece of paper from my pocket and put it down on the counter in front of him. "This car was rented here a couple of weeks ago." I pointed to the space where C. Weiss was written in pen. "Is it normal you don't use a full name on a car rental?"

He picked up the paper and looked it up and down. He handed it back to me and shrugged. "Things are kind of laid back here. It's how we do business...make it easy to rent a car without the hassle. Especially if you don't have good credit or want to pay cash. Or if you need to rent for just a few hours."

"A few hours?"

He nodded. "Sometimes." He looked past me at Alex. "It costs a little more to do it that way, but people like the option."

"What if someone pays cash but doesn't return the car?"

Tyler shrugged. "Our insurance covers it."

"Why bother with paperwork? Sounds like it's a cash exchange and a handshake."

"Paperwork's required by the insurance company," he said.

I said, "Are you pretty strict about IDs?"

Tyler shook his head. "No. Not really."

"So someone could come here, pay up the cash, give you a fake ID—or none at all—and be able to rent a car? I'm surprised you get the cars back at all."

"We tend to work with people in a...uh...network."

"A network?" I said. "What kind of network?"

He shrugged. "People we're familiar with."

I hadn't paid much attention the first time I was there to the framed photos on the wall behind him. But this time I looked closer. One of the photos was of Frank Sinatra. Another of The World Trade Center. There was a framed photo of Derek Jeter.

"Are you from New York?" I said.

He looked over his shoulder at the wall. "No sir. The owner's from New York. He lives up there."

"He doesn't live here? In Florida?"

"Well, I guess he has a house here, but he spends most of his time in New York. He's got other businesses."

"Is his last name Darcy?"

"No. It's DiGiacomo. Nick DiGiacomo." He moved papers around behind the counter and looked toward the door. He seemed to be getting antsy with my questions. "He hasn't been in here in a few weeks."

I pushed the paper in front of Tyler again and pointed to the name. "Do you know this name?"

"Weiss?"

"C. Weiss."

Tyler leaned over a computer and tapped the keyboard. "Where'd you get this?" He held upu the paper.

I said, "Does it matter?"

Tyler gave me a look like he wasn't about to let me push him around. "It might," he said.

"It was the young woman who helped me. She gave it to me."

"Emma?" He shook his head. "Emma wouldn't give this to you." His voice was a bit uneven, like he was getting nervous.

I shrugged. "I guess I don't know where I got it then."

Tyler's gaze shifted to the phone on the counter. "I can't answer any more of your questions. I'm sorry, but I think I need to ask you to leave."

"I'm not trying to cause you any problems, Tyler."

He said, "Well, the thing is, the officers asked me to call them if anyone came around who seemed suspicious."

I put my hands up, like I'd surrendered. "I'm not suspicious. I'm just a private investigator. I'm not here to cause trouble." I reached into my pocket and pulled out my card. "Here." I placed it down on the counter.

Tyler picked it up and looked it over, nodding. "Okay. Look. That car rental, I remember the guy who rented it. Someone called in for it, to reserve it, and said the name was C. Weiss."

"Male or female?"

"Female."

"Did a woman pick up the car?"

He shook his head. "I don't think so. Just the one guy came, but I think there was someone else out in the car."

"Didn't you get an ID or anything?"

Tyler shook his head. He started to open his mouth like he was going to say something, but stopped.

I looked up at the camera on the wall. "Does that camera film in here all day?"

He turned, looked behind him and shook his head. "No, that one doesn't work."

Alex said, "Are there any other cameras?"

"Just the one outside. It's not a very good one. I don't know if we even have it on." Tyler took a deep swallow. "As far as I know, the cops didn't find anything on it."

I turned back toward Alex. "Stone say anything about it?"

"About watching the footage?" She shook her head. "I'm not sure he'd tell me if he did."

I turned back to Tyler. "Any chance you'd let us look through the video? I promise...we won't take anything. If we can just take a quick look, Alex knows how to plow through this stuff, maybe see something the cops overlooked."

Tyler looked past us toward the exit, scratching his head. "Make it fast though. My manager shows up, I'll be—"

"Give us ten minutes and we'll be out of your way." I handed him a twenty dollar bill. He looked at my hand without taking the bribe. I pulled another twenty out of my pocket and handed him two bills.

He took the money and stuck it in his pants pocket. "There's an office in back, around the corner. You'll see the desk against the wall with the monitor."

Alex walked behind the counter and into the back room.

I gave Tyler a nod and followed her into the back room. I looked down at the spot where I first saw the poor, young girl lying lifeless on the concrete floor. "We can't take all day," I said to Alex.

She walked into the small office and sat down at the desk with the computer. She tapped on the keyboard and clicked the mouse, moving around the screen.

I watched over her shoulder.

Within a few moments she had the footage from the day before Philip's boat exploded. She looked at the monitor and said, "What time does it say on that slip...when they came in for the rental?"

"Four-twenty."

She typed on the keyboard and we watched the footage jump from one camera to the next, from interior to exterior, front to back. "There," she said.

Two men stepped out of a black Lincoln Town Car. Neither was dressed for the beach, both wore black with long dress pants and short sleeves.

"You can barely make out their faces," I said. "What about the driver? Can you see a face?"

"Hard to see," Alex said. "If I had to guess, it looks like a female."

"Yeah?" I leaned closer to the monitor. "Can you zoom in?"

Alex reached into her backpack and pulled out a small, metal box.

"What's that?"

"Portable harddrive. I'm going to look at this at home...this monitor's resolution is a joke." She looked behind her, toward the door. "Make sure Tyler doesn't come in here."

"Can you fit everything on there?"

She nodded. "I'll take as much as I can." She plugged the hard drive into the computer and continued moving the computer's mouse around the screen while the files were copied over. She zoomed in closer toward the front of the car in the parking lot, shaking her head. "I can't make out the face. Not yet."

Chapter 33

ALEX DROPPED ME OFF at Billy's Place. And as I stepped out
of her Jeep, I said "You sure you don't want to come in for a
quick drink?"

She shook her head. "I need to get home. Raz has been alone
all day."

"You'll be home later?" I said.

"I have some things I need to do. I'll go through the footage
as soon as I can, see if I can get a clear picture of who was
driving that car."

I paused for a moment. "I hope it wasn't Philip."

"Why would it've been? You really think he could've set this
whole thing up?"

I looked at her but didn't have much of an answer. "I don't
know what to think. But as soon as you see anything on that
film, call me right away."

• • • • • • • • •

Billy came over as soon as I sat down at the bar. He tossed his towel over his shoulder. "Your friend was in here looking for you."

"I don't have many, so you'd think it'd be easy for me to guess who you're talking about."

Billy put a glass in front of me. "Are you still thinking about going on the wagon?"

I shook my head. "Not today."

He poured me a shot. "It was Kathleen who was here. She said she'd come back tonight. But I told her I didn't know if you'd be here or not. She said she'd been trying to catch up with you."

I reached into my pocket and pulled out my phone. I hadn't missed any calls. "What else did she say?"

Billy shrugged. "She was pretty short with me."

I turned, looked at the door. Part of me wanted to see her walk in. The other part hoped I'd never see her again. It'd be for the better. "Alex and I went by Darcy Car Rental. Kid working there let us look at their security footage."

"The cops didn't do that?"

"They did. But it had to do with that poor girl's death, not to find out who was driving the car I saw at the marina."

Billy reached for his cup and took a sip. "What'd you find out?"

I picked up my glass, held it up under my chin as I spoke. "Alex thinks it looked like a woman behind the wheel of the car out front of Darcy Car Rental...the evening before the explosion."

"A woman, huh?" Billy looked down at me as he wiped the inside of a glass with his towel.

I gave him a look and sipped my drink. "Alex is looking at it tonight, from home. Hopefully she can get a cleaner look. But I don't know if she'll have much luck. From what I saw it was like looking through glasses in the rain."

"Maybe it was your friend, Carla Weiss?"

I shook my head. "Maybe. That would make sense with everything that happened. And, of course, it's her name—at least her initial—on the invoice."

Billy looked toward the entrance. "Why would she use her real name?"

I turned in my seat. Kathleen walked toward me with a much different look than the one she had the last few times I saw her. Her hair was down, she didn't have any makeup on her face. It was hard to tell, but it almost looked as if she was crying.

I turned and looked at Billy as he gave me a look and walked away.

Kathleen put her hand on my arm and stepped between me and the stool next to me. "Is this seat taken?"

I sipped my Jack and shook my head without answering. "You okay?"

She didn't answer, but put her finger up toward Billy. "May I have a glass of chardonnay?"

"Would you like to see the wine list?" he said.

"No, whatever you pour will do the job just fine."

I had one elbow on the bar, my glass up near my mouth. I stared straight ahead. "I thought our little game was over."

She sat on the stool. "My husband has left the country. He's gone to Italy."

That got my attention, but I still didn't say a word. I turned and glanced at her.

"His attorney contacted me this morning, said he agreed to sign the divorce papers. I was scheduled to fly out today but, after we spoke, I decided to stay one more night."

Billy put a glass of chardonnay down in front of Kathleen. She picked it up, raised her glass to me, and took a sip.

I lifted my glass off the bar, tipped my head back and threw what was left down my throat. Billy had the bottle ready—like he read my mind—and filled my glass with another shot.

I turned to Kathleen. "I don't know if I understand exactly what you're looking for."

"What part don't you understand?"

"You were pretty clear your husband wasn't going to let you divorce him. Now you come in here, tell me he's left the country?" I sat staring across the bar, my glass in my hand. "You can stay if you'd like, but if you do I'm going to pay my tab and get going."

Whatever smile Kathleen had on her face quickly disappeared. She pulled her purse from behind her stool and tucked it under her arm. She stood, reached into her purse, and pulled out a twenty she tossed on the bar.

I picked it up and handed it back to her. "My treat."

She looked off for a moment, turned to me and said, "I heard about your friend, Philip. I just wanted to say I'm sorry." She stopped, turned and walked out the door.

Billy walked over to me and leaned with his hands down on the bar. He opened his mouth as if to say something, but stopped. He took her glass of wine and tossed what was left in the sink. He said, "It takes a lot of willpower to turn away someone that beautiful. Even if she is a little crazy."

I turned and looked over my shoulder toward the door, wondering if I made a mistake. I pushed my glass toward Billy. "Did I hear her say something about Philip?"

I nodded. "Gave her condolences, I guess."

"How'd she know him?"

I shrugged. "We got together one night in Ocracoke. He flew in on his helicopter one night, with Victoria."

Chapter 34

I SLOWLY EASED OUT of a Jack Daniels-induced coma, looking out the window. It was still dark out, and my first thought was that sleeping upstairs from a bar owned by my best friend might not be the best idea.

I started to close my eyes when my phone rang. I answered and barely got out a hello.

It was Alex.

"Are you awake?" she said.

I sat up on the edge of the couch. "What's up?"

"I was out with Mike Stone last night."

I thought for a moment. "Please tell me he's not there next to you..."

There was quiet on the other end. I knew right away it was the wrong thing to say.

She said, "Knock it off, will you? Just listen to me for a minute. It's Philip. He's not dead. That wasn't his body in the car at the airport."

That woke me up.

"How do you know?"

"Mike got the call last night, when we were out."

"What'd he say?"

"It was Philip's brother."

"Frank?"

"He had Philip's wallet in his pocket. His license, credit cards..."

"You think he was at the airport with Philip?"

"Well, there was no record of Philip on any plane to Sydney."

"So he never left?"

"The only record they found was Frank's. There was a one-way ticket to Sydney."

"But it wasn't Frank?" I said. "Jesus, that's how he did it. They swapped ID's."

• • • ● • ● • • •

Alex was already at a table at the Java Jazz Cafe when I walked in. She had a coffee ready for me and slid it across the table as I sat down. "Mike said it was set up to look like a suicide. He said whoever did it didn't do a very good job."

"I still can't believe it." I glanced down at my phone. "I wish I knew how to get in touch with him."

"Philip?"

I nodded.

"Mike said he didn't have much else. In fact he cut the night short once he got the call."

"Did you talk to him this morning?"

"No. Not yet. He said..." Alex stopped what she was about to say.

"He said what?"

She stared back at me for a moment. "He tried to tell me not to tell you anything until he knew more. I told him if he didn't want you to know he shouldn't have told me in the first place."

I smiled. "I bet that went over well."

Alex shrugged and sipped her tea, holding her mug with both hands.

We both sat quiet for a moment. I sipped my coffee, not feeling well at all. As much as I needed a few drinks the night before, I had a sense of guilt or dread or something that was digging into me. The truth was, my hangovers were always drowned in guilt. But it felt worse than that.

"You think Mike'll look at Philip as a suspect?"

"For Frank's death?" She shook her head. "Like I said, he didn't want to go into it. And he left me with the bill."

"And they're sure it was Philip's car?"

Alex nodded. "It was a BMW registered to him. Keys were in the ignition." She looked me over. "Are you okay?"

I didn't answer. "Did you look at the tape?"

"From Darcy's? Didn't you get my message?"

I said, "You left me a message?"

"I did. Late last night."

"Oh, I could've—" I pulled out my phone and turned it toward Alex. "Here it is. Like I said...rough night."

"I did all I could," she said. "But it's impossible to see who it is. I can almost guarantee it's a woman. I sent it off to Carson to see if he can do anything else with it. If he can't clean it up to see if we can get an ID, nobody can. I sent him Carla's photo, too. At the very least, maybe he can make a match..."

I looked around at the crowd, starting to build up with men and women lined up out the door for coffee, most dressed in their business-like outfits. I felt pity...their heads down in their phones, waiting to get gassed up on caffeine so they can make it through another day in a cubicle or in long meetings.

I'd rather put a bullet in my head.

I sipped my coffee. "Kathleen showed up at Billy's last night."

"Is that why you're in the condition you're in today?"

I shrugged. "I was on my way long before she got there. Although she might've pushed me over the edge. She didn't even finish her glass of wine before she walked out."

She huffed out a laugh. "Sounds like it went well."

"I think we're done for good," I said. "Much better off...I think you know that."

Alex looked down into her mug of tea. "If she was so into you, why'd she disappear in the first place?"

I didn't respond, because I didn't have a good enough answer.

Alex sipped her tea and looked at me over the rim.

"She knew about Philip," I said. "Or, I should say, she knew Philip was dead...before he wasn't."

"What's that mean?"

I shrugged. "I don't know. I didn't ask. Maybe she heard it on the news?"

Alex shook her head. "It wasn't on the news. At least I don't think it was."

"Maybe something online? I don't know. You know how things are nowadays. News travels fast. But Billy got me thinking about something, after he asked me how she knew him."

"Didn't they meet in Ocracoke?" she said.

I nodded. "We spent some time together...the four of us. Victoria was with him."

"And how'd you actually meet her in the first place?"

I smiled. "She came up to me at a bar."

"Just out of the blue?"

"Why, hard to believe someone picked me up?"

"No, that's not what I'm saying..."

I stared back at her. "What are you saying?"

Alex leaned back in her chair and looked past me for a moment. "I don't know. Nothing, I guess."

Before Alex could say another word, my phone vibrated in my pocket. I pulled it out and looked at the screen. "It's Billy."

Alex's phone rang just as I was saying hello. She put her finger up to me and mouthed that it was Mike Stone. She got up from the table and walked outside.

I stayed in my seat. "Billy?"

"Henry...thank god, you're alive."

"I know I overdid it last night, but—"

"No, listen. Please...I thought you were upstairs." Billy's voice shook.

I knew something was wrong.

"My restaurant. It's gone."

"What do you mean it's gone?" I felt a chill rip through my spine.

"There was an explosion. It just happened, maybe twenty minutes ago. The whole thing is gone. My restaurant...there's nothing left."

Billy was always one for forming perfect sentences, but I could hear it in his voice he was far out of character...the way the words flowed—or didn't flow—from his mouth.

220

"The fire department's still trying to put it out." His voice cracked. "I thought you were upstairs."

"You mean, you thought I was..."

"I was sure you were still asleep. After all those drinks." The phone went quiet. "I thought you were dead."

I leaned on the table with my head in my hand, the phone still up to my ear. "Billy, what the hell happened?"

"There was an explosion. The restaurant is gone."

Chapter 35

BILLY, ALEX AND I sat in the sheriff's office having a face-to-face with Mike Stone and a few select members of the Bomb Squad.

Mike held his styrofoam cup of coffee up under his chin. "I don't think any of us has any doubt at this stage you're the target." He took a sip and put the cup down on the table. "Your boat. Your car. And as I understand, your temporary sleeping quarters above the restaurant." Mike shook his head. "Looks like I'm not the only one who doesn't like you." He turned to Billy. "Probably regret offering him your couch, huh?"

Billy said to Mike, "Sorry, I don't get your humor. All I can say is I'm happy my friend's alive."

Mike squinted his eyes, staring back at Billy. "You seem to be taking this all quite well. For someone who just lost his business..."

"Are you implying I had something to do with it? Because you're right. You got me...I blew the place up. I did the boat, too. And the car, too."

I looked at Billy and gave him a nod.

· · · ● · ● · ● · · ·

The three of us walked down the steps of the sheriff's office and headed across the parking lot toward Billy's car. I walked around to the passenger side and across the roof said, "I'm really sorry, Billy. I know this is all my fault."

Billy shook his head. "You're not the one who destroyed my restaurant."

"You know what I mean," I said. "As Mike made so clear, it was obviously meant for me."

"Listen," Billy said. "Maybe it's a blessing...for the best. Insurance will cover it. I'm just glad you're alive." He opened his door and stepped inside. "Besides, maybe it gives me a fresh start."

"That's quite a glass-is-half-full way to look at it." I buckled myself into the passenger seat. "I hope that means you'll reopen."

Billy shrugged. "Who knows. Maybe I'll get out of the restaurant business."

Alex was already sitting in the back seat looking at her phone but looked up at Billy. "Did you just say you might get out of the restaurant business?"

He looked back at her and smiled. "Just a thought."

I said to Alex. "We need to dig as deep as we can into everyone's past, find a link to explosives. I don't know if it's military or what, but..."

"You still think Philip is behind this?" Billy said.

I shook my head. "I could see him blowing up his own boat. He'd just get a new one. But he wouldn't do it if it'd harm someone. And I'd like to think he wouldn't want to kill me." I looked out the passenger window. "At least I'd like to think he wouldn't."

Billy turned onto North Liberty and took a quick left onto East Bay.

I turned again to Alex. "Can you check with your friend...see if he's had a chance to look at the footage from Darcy Car Rental."

She looked down at her phone and dialed. "Hey," she said. "It's Alex. Just wondering if you...You did? I haven't checked. Okay, yes. Uh huh. Makes sense. I'll check now. I appreciate it."

"Anything?" I said, as I turned and looked at Alex over my shoulder.

"He said he did what he could, but couldn't find a match in the database."

I said, "Did you send him the picture of Carla?"

"Yes, but he said the footage isn't clear enough to make a match."

• • • • • • • • • •

Alex and I drove together out to Neptune Beach and parked in front of the leasing office at Carla's apartment. I knew Carla was gone, but hoped someone might provide us a clue about where we could find her.

"I'll tell them I'm looking for a place," I said. "Pretty sure Carla's is vacant."

Alex said, "Would you really want to live all the way out here?"

"Why not? I like the beach. And a change wouldn't be such a bad thing."

We walked into the leasing office. A young woman looked up at us from behind a desk and stood from her chair, walked toward us with her hand extended and shook our hands. "Hello," she said. "I'm CeCe. How may I help you two?"

"CeCe?" I said.

She nodded.

"I'm looking for an apartment. A friend of mine told me you might have a vacancy on the third floor?"

She put on a big smile. "When are you looking to move in?"

I looked through the blinds covering the window, and spotted a sign on the post outside. It said Beach Path with an arrow pointing toward the back of the building. "How about today?"

She laughed. "Well, the soonest we have available is a couple of weeks." CeCe looked at me and Alex. "I don't think I can show you the home just yet. Not right now. It's only been recently vacated. It's being refurbished." She held the back of her hand up near her mouth, like she was letting us in on a secret. "I probably shouldn't tell you this, but someone smashed the sliding glass door off the balcony. It's being repaired."

I glanced back at Alex. "Must have had some rowdy tenants," I said. "But I don't mind if it's being worked on. I'd love to see it, since I drove all the way out here." I spotted a board with dozens of keys hanging on hooks. "Does it have a view?"

She nodded. "Third floor...one of the nicest in the building. It's overlooking the beach."

"So why'd she move out?"

The smile dropped from her face. "How'd you know the tenant was a she?"

"Oh, a woman lived there?"

CeCe had a tilt to her head, stared back at me for a moment then said. "She was nice. Kind of caught me off guard she was leaving...still had three months on her lease."

"She broke the lease?"

"Yes, but it was paid in full." She looked back at Alex and raised her eyebrows. "Paid in cash."

"How long ago'd she leave?"

"Officially? This morning." CeCe looked up at the clock on the wall behind her desk. "I'd say about three hours ago."

"When she left, did you see who she left with?"

CeCe folded her arms. "I'm sorry. But you're asking a lot of questions that aren't exactly what we hear from someone looking to move in here."

I shot Alex a quick look, turned back to CeCe and said, "The truth is, I like the area. And I am looking for a place." I handed her my card. "I'm a private investigator."

"What are you investigating?"

"I'm looking for your former tenant, Carla Weiss."

CeCe swallowed hard and looked toward the door. "You know, I didn't know her very well. She kept to herself. And today, when she was leaving—after she came in to tell me—I saw a kid she was with. I swear I went to high school with him, down in St. Augustine."

"You're not from around here?"

She shook her head. "I moved here after high school. To work here." She stood quiet for a moment.

"So this kid she was with...anything you can tell us?"

Her face got a bit twisted as she shrugged. "I don't know...he was a black kid. Not that I mean anything by that. I'm just saying. He was one of the smarter kids in my school. Kind of a nerd, I guess. But he got expelled and I never saw him again."

Alex said, "You remember his name?"

"Like I said, maybe it wasn't him. The boy I knew...his name was Jason Raymond."

I looked at Alex. "Jason Raymond?"

She stared back at me for a moment, then realized what I'd already figured out. "JayRay?"

I nodded. "It had to be. Jason Raymond is JayRay."

Alex turned to the young woman, "You know what he got expelled for?"

She shook her head. "It was kind of a big deal at the time. He made a bomb."

Chapter 36

ALEX TOOK THE JEEP down A1A, turned west onto 202 then headed southbound on 295. We'd hoped to catch Julie Sanders at the Gem and Mineral Society since she seemed to be the only person not missing.

I turned to Alex. "I wonder how the hell Jayray ended up with Carla."

"We can't be sure it was him," she said.

"Of *course* it was him."

"Maybe Carla's been playing all sides. Turned on Philip...turned on Frank. Jayray would've known what Frank was up to the whole time."

"When we were at Carla's, Frank's holding the gun on Carla. Jayray's playing it kind of a little too cool. The most he did was pistol whipped me, cracked me right on the side of the head. Otherwise...the more I think about it, it makes sense it was all for show. He just happens to escape, leaves Frank for dead on the ground."

"You think he'd been working with Carla all this time?" Alex said.

I shrugged. "I have no idea."

We pulled down the road leading to the Gem and Mineral Society's building and Alex slammed on the brakes as we turned the corner, the building within view. There were three vehicles from the sheriff's office and an EMS vehicle backed-up toward the front door.

I stood up inside the Jeep and looked through a pair of binoculars and watched someone get wheeled out on a gurney. "It's Annie, the old lady."

Alex spotted a friend of hers, Chris Carson, an officer she'd gone through the police academy with. He was standing at the front of the building. "I'll go ask him what's going on," she said as she stepped down from the Jeep and walked toward the crowd.

I followed after her. Officer Chris Carson stared at us as we walked toward him.

"Alex? What are you doing here?"

She turned and looked at me before she answered. "Uh, we were just driving by. Henry's actually a member, so he was concerned it might be someone he knows."

Chris gave me a look that said he wasn't buying Alex's answer.

I nodded. "I'm a big collector." I looked toward the gurney, saw that it was Annie—the old lady—being pushed into the back of the EMS vehicle. I nodded toward her and said, "What happened?"

Chris took a moment before he answered. "She fell down the steps out back, trying to get away."

Two other officers walked out with Julie Sanders, her hands cuffed behind her back. She looked right at me, her teeth clenched. "Did you have anything to do with this?"

I didn't answer.

Chris turned to me. "Are you going to tell me what she meant by that?"

I shrugged, shaking my head. "I have no idea."

Alex said, "Can you tell us what happened?"

Chris slowly started to nod. "She'd been stealing jewels from members...replaced whatever she took with fakes."

Alex said, "Is it okay if we go inside...have a look around?"

He paused. "Why don't you just tell me the truth? You weren't really just driving by, were you..."

Alex gave him a slight smile. "We'll only be a few minutes."

He looked around and took a deep breath. "Make it fast. And don't touch anything."

We walked through the open door. A couple of officers stood around talking, but didn't seem to be doing much else. Another officer in plain clothes with a badge on his belt watched us as we walked in. A woman who appeared to be in charge told two younger officers what to do as they carried cardboard boxes out the front door.

I looked for the wooden crate but didn't see anything that even resembled what Carla and Dominic had dropped off.

Alex walked ahead of me and slipped through a doorway. She said, "Henry...in here."

Alex was in a small room reaching under a long table. She pulled on a blanket and revealed the wooden crate.

"Is that it?" I said.

She looked back at me over her shoulder and lifted the wooden top off the crate. She reached her hand inside and pulled out a black velvet bag. It was tied tight with a gold string.

She handed it to me and I untied the string. I looked inside. "Are these diamonds?" I reached inside the bag and showed her what I'd pulled from the bag.

Alex reached inside the crate and pulled out another velvet bag.

I looked behind me at the door and made sure nobody was coming in the room. "Should I close the door?"

She shook her head. "That'll attract attention." She struggled to slide the crate out from under the table, just enough to get her head over the top. She looked inside. "There must be twenty more bags like this."

"How do we know if they're real?" I said.

Alex didn't answer but grabbed the bags from my hands and stuck them back in the crate. "Let's cover this up before someone walks in."

"They're cleaning this place out. They're going to take them," I said. "We should keep a bag. I don't mean we keep the diamonds...but see if—"

One of the officers stuck his head in the small room. He looked back and forth at me and Alex. "*Who the hell are you? What are you two doing here?*" His hand was close to his holster.

"I'm Henry Walsh. This is my associate, Alex Jepson. We're with Walsh Investigations."

The officer took a step closer and looked at the crate under the table. Alex had already slipped the blanket over it.

"I don't give two shits about who you're with. I asked you what you're doing. This is a crime scene, under investigation by the Jacksonville Sheriff's Office."

I opened my mouth to speak as officer Carson stepped in behind the young officer. "Everything okay?"

"I caught these two snooping around. No idea how they even got in here. I think we ought to—"

"They're okay, officer. They have permission to be here." Chris was a big man who towered over the shorter, younger officer. "Why don't you go help officer Knox move the rest of those boxes out to the truck?"

"Yes, sir," he said. The officer turned and left the room without saying another word.

Chris waited a moment. "Are you going to tell me what's going on?"

Alex shook her head. "We were just talking...came in here so we could discuss something in private."

Chris gave an unconvincing nod. "Well, we're done here. Recovered what was reported stolen." He looked down at the blanket covering the crate. "Please keep yourselves out of tr ouble." He turned to leave the room and stopped just outside the doorway. "Come on, we gotta lock up."

Alex and I gave each other a look then followed him out of the building.

Outside, I said, "Chris."

He stopped in the driveway and looked back at me.

"What was Julie Sanders involved in? Do you know what it was she was stealing?"

Chris looked over at the boxes being loaded into the truck. "Rare gems...worth quite a bit of money."

"You know the name?"

"The name?"

"Who she stole from?"

He shook his head. "No. We received an anonymous call."

Chapter 37

IT WAS LATE INTO the night when Alex and I went back to the Jacksonville Gem and Mineral Society. We parked up on the hill, as we did earlier.

Alex leaned on the hood of her Jeep with binoculars up against her face. "How are we supposed to get in?"

"Assuming there's an alarm, that's a good question," I said. I reached under my seat and pulled out a flashlight. "Or we break a window and get what we need before the cops show up."

Alex removed the binoculars from her face. "You really think this is a good idea?"

"Probably not. But I need to see if there's anything we missed, buried in that crate." I stepped from the Jeep and started down the hill.

Alex followed and we both stopped when we noticed headlights reflecting off the building. We crouched down behind the row of shrubs.

A black car—the Lincoln Town Car—pulled up in front of the building. Carla stepped out of the driver's side and closed the door behind her. She looked around and her gaze passed right over me and Alex.

The back door opened and Annie—the old lady who'd only a few hours earlier been taken away in an EMS vehicle—stepped from the back of the car. She handed Carla a flashlight and Carla walked away, shining the light toward an area behind the building.

She walked to a shed tucked under some live oaks.

Annie walked up to the front door, walked inside the building, and closed the door behind her. A light went on inside.

Carla was at the shed with the flashlight and opened the doors.

A white van drove down the driveway and stopped behind the Lincoln. The driver's door opened and Jayray stepped out. He walked around the back, pulled open the doors and reached inside. He pulled out a woman who appeared with a black hood over her head.

In a whisper, Alex said, "Who is it?"

"I don't know. It's too dark."

She reached behind her back and handed me her Glock. "Where's the 9mm?"

"In the Jeep," I said.

"Be right back," she said as she stayed low and made her way up the hill to the Jeep, came back and crouched down beside me. She handed me the 9mm.

It was hard to see, but I could tell the woman Jayray pulled from the van had her hands tied behind her back. He held one of her arms and walked with her toward the shed.

I took a few steps closer and stopped behind a wide, old live oak. It was dark enough outside that I didn't think they could see us. The only light came from the flashlight in Carla's hand. She stood in front of the shed, watching Jayray walk toward her with the woman.

Jayray stopped and Carla took the woman by the arm and pulled her into the shed.

I turned and looked back at Alex, still behind the shrubs.

There was a distinctive click behind my head followed by a cold, hard muzzle jammed into the back of my skull. The voice from the man behind me said, "Where's your gun?" He pulled Alex's gun from my pants. "Come on out, sweetie."

Alex stood up from behind the shrubs with her hands in the air.

The man had a gun on each of us.

The man, I knew as soon as I heard him speak, was Dominic.

"Is that Philip's fiancé?" I said.

"Shut up," he said. He gestured with the guns for us to move out of the wooded area and toward the driveway. "Why don't you go see for yourself?" He shoved me ahead of him.

Alex and I stood side-by-side outside the rear doors of the van. I looked over toward the shed.

Dominic yelled, "Carla, your boyfriend's here."

Carla stuck her head out the doors of the shed. "Told you we'd see him here," she said. She walked toward us. "Oh, Henry, part of me honestly thinks it's good to see you." She turned to Alex. "He's such a good looking man. You're lucky." Then looked back at me. "Or should I say...was lucky." She yelled toward the shed. "Jayray, grab some more rope."

I looked at Carla. "Is it Victoria?"

She paused, shaking her head. "Good guess. But I'm sorry. You're wrong." She walked to her car and reached inside through the open driver's side window, reaching for a pack of cigarettes from the dashboard. She took one out and lit it with her hand cupped over the flame, took a drag and blew the smoke into the air.

Jayray walked out of the shed and gave me a nod when he saw me.

I looked at Carla. "Isn't he a little young for you?"

Carla smiled, the cigarette between her two long fingers up near her face. "You mean, my boy toy?" She shook her head. "No, not my thing."

Jayray grabbed my arms as Dominic stepped in closer with the gun still pointed at my head. Jayray wrapped the rope around my wrists.

He moved over to Alex and grabbed her hands. He lifted her shirt. "What's this?" he said. He pulled her Glock from the back of her pants. Jayray looked up at Dominic. "You even check to make sure nobody was carrying?" Jayray looked over at Carla. "Told you he was a dope."

I could hear Dominic's breathing getting heavier. He turned the gun from me and Alex and swung it hard against Jayray's head.

Jayray dropped to the ground.

Carla stared back at Dominic. "What the hell are you doing?" She pulled her own gun on him. "You have to control that temper, man. He's just a kid." She leaned over, grabbed the rope from Jayray's limp hand and finished tying Alex's wrists together.

The door to the building opened and the old lady, Annie, walked out carrying a case in each hand and one tucked under her arm. "What the hell's going on?" she said. She looked down toward me, my arms tied behind my back, seated on the ground next to Alex. She turned to Carla. "Where'd you get these two?"

I watched Annie come down the steps and walk to the car. She popped the trunk and placed the cases she was carrying inside. She didn't appear nearly as old as she had when we'd first met. She said, "Did he see his girlfriend yet?"

Carla shook her head.

Jayray got up from the ground and rubbed his head where Dominic cracked him with the pistol.

The old lady walked with Carla toward the shed, stepped inside, and came right back out holding their hostage by the arm. She pulled her toward us and ripped off the hood.

My heart stopped when I saw who it was. "Kathleen?"

Chapter 38

KATHLEEN, ALEX, AND I were tied-up and locked inside the shed. The windows were boarded-up with plywood. And other than thin slits of light slipping through the cracks, it was impossible to see anything at all.

The voices outside grew louder. There was yelling.

And then a single gunshot.

Nobody said a word as both engines started, followed by the sounds of tires moving over gravel. The sound from the cars faded until it was quiet.

I couldn't see her, but Kathleen said, "They're just going to leave us here?"

I didn't answer her as I struggled to get free from the rope tied around my wrists. It sounded like Alex was doing the same.

"Kathleen?" I said. "How did they get you?"

"I was outside my hotel waiting for a cab. A man came up to me, said he had a gun and told me to get in the car. He told me to be quiet or he'd shoot me dead."

"Did anyone tell you why?" I said, my voice uneven as I worked at getting loose.

"Because you wouldn't back off."

I stopped for a moment. "That's what he told you?"

Kathleen said, "Said I was their insurance, that you'd stay out of their way."

Alex said, "Did you hear anything else?"

All three of us were quiet.

I waited for her to answer. "Kathleen?"

She said, "Oh, were you asking me?"

"Alex asked if you heard them say anything about what they're doing," I said. "Or anything that'll help us."

"I think they're trying to catch a plane."

Alex said, "All of them?"

Kathleen paused. "I'm not sure."

I finally got my hands loose and got up on my feet. I stepped toward the door and led with my shoulder into the doors. They opened with a loud bang. I stood in the doorway and rubbed my shoulder, turned out toward the driveway and in the distance saw a body on the ground. "It's Dominic," I said. "I think he's been shot."

"There's a knife up in my Jeep," Alex said.

I ran up the hill and grabbed the knife from her center console, then went back in the shed and cut Alex free.

"Is he dead?" she said.

"Let's get us out of here first."

I sliced through the ropes around Alex's wrists, then cut Kathleen free.

I said to her, "I thought you were leaving?"

The sounds of sirens screamed in the distance, growing louder as they seemed to be moving closer.

"Let's go," I said as the three of us walked from the shed.

Alex turned and looked toward Dominic, face down in the driveway. "What about him?"

"We need to get out of here," I said.

• • • • • • • • • •

Alex was behind the wheel, not saying much at all on the way to Billy's house.

Kathleen was in the back.

I turned my head over my shoulder and looked at her. "When I first saw you with your head covered, I'd hoped you were Victoria."

Kathleen stared back at me. "I don't know how I'm supposed to take that, but..."

The three of us were quiet.

I turned to Alex. "We still have nothing. No answers. I can't make sense of anything."

She gave me a quick look. "Not yet. But we're getting there, don't you think? Dominic might be dead. And Carla and her mother are clearly..."

"We don't know what Carla and her mother's roles are," I said. "Looks to me they sold diamonds to Julie and, for some reason...stole them back. And there's a good chance none of this has anything to do with Philip *or* Victoria."

Alex turned the wheel and pulled the Jeep to the front of Billy's garage.

He stood outside on his porch, watching as we stepped out. With his voice lowered, he said, "Chloe's here, too. She had a fight with Jake, asked if she could stay here for the night."

I turned and gestured toward Kathleen. "Billy, you remember Kathleen?"

He gave me a look, then nodded toward her with a smile I knew was forced. "Of course I do." He held the door open and let Alex and Kathleen walk in ahead of us. I stopped just outside the door. "I appreciate you letting her stay here. I just need to keep her safe..."

Billy put his hand on my back and guided me through the door without a word.

Chloe leaned with her elbows on the island in the kitchen, talking to Kathleen and Alex. She smiled when she saw me walk in. "Hey, Henry." She came over and gave me a hug. "I have something for you."

"A gift?"

She gave me a look. "Didn't you get my message?"

I pulled my phone from my pocket. "It's dead."

Alex said, "He won't listen to them even when the battery's good."

"Let me get it," Chloe said as she walked out of the kitchen and up the stairs.

She came back to the kitchen a moment later with a manilla envelope. "A man dropped this off for you the other night."

Billy looked at her. "The other night?"

Chloe looked at Henry. "I'm sorry. He said it was for Henry and nobody else."

"What'd he look like?" I said.

She shrugged. "Older man. White hair, bald in the front...shirt untucked...had one of those big pot bellies."

Alex and I looked at each other.

"Charles."

Everyone watched as I opened the envelope. Inside was a key attached to a keychain with a plastic tag on it. The tag had Rebel Storage printed on it. There was a number written in black marker on the back. I read the number out loud. "One-seven-eight-six." I had no idea what it was. I looked inside the envelope for something else, but there was nothing. Just the key in a big, oversized envelope. "You sure there wasn't anything else?"

Chloe nodded.

I pulled my phone from my pocket and remembered my phone was dead. "Billy, any chance you have a charger?"

He nodded and walked through the front door.

Kathleen stepped closer to me. "Do you have any idea what it's for?"

"The key?" I shook my head. "Honestly, I have no idea. If I had to guess..."

I glanced at Alex, who had her eyes on Kathleen standing a little too close to me.

Alex looked away when she noticed me watching her.

"You know where it is?" Kathleen said.

"Rebel Storage." I shook my head.

Kathleen put her hand on top of mine. "Maybe we should take a ride, go check it out."

I looked up just as Alex was rolling her eyes. "Probably best you stay here with Billy. Alex and I will go."

Billy came through the front door with a black wire dangling from his hand. He handed me a charger. "This should work."

Alex smirked at Kathleen. "You'll be safe here."

Chapter 39

I PULLED MY CAR into the parking lot of Rebel Storage, in Westside. Alex and I stopped in front of the closed steel gate at the front entrance. The keypad just before the gate indicated the only way inside was with a code.

I didn't *have* a code.

I flipped the key tag over to make sure I hadn't overlooked a number. But there was nothing. I pulled the folded envelope from my pocket and looked inside.

No code.

I turned to Alex, shaking my head. "This isn't good."

My phone rang with a number I didn't recognize. I answered, "Walsh Investigations."

The voice on the other end said, "You bring me the sculpture. I'll bring you Victoria."

"Who is this?"

"It doesn't matter who it is. Bring me the pelican."

"What makes you think I have it?"

"Keep it up and you'll see what happens to the fiancé."

I looked down at the key in my hand. "But I don't have it."

The caller's voice was one I didn't recognize. He paused a moment before he continued. "Then *get* the damn pelican. And when I call you again, you'd better have it. I'll tell you then where to deliver it."

"If you're telling me the truth and you really have Victoria..." I realized the caller had hung up.

I turned to Alex. "Unless whoever just called was lying, Victoria's not in Sydney. And, if I had to guess, the crystal pelican is inside this storage unit. If it is, then I was just told to deliver it."

"Why would we do that?" Alex said.

"He said we'd get Victoria back. And I'm not taking any chances this time. We've gotta get inside." I looked through the gate and along the chain link fence that enclosed the entire facility. "Somehow."

We walked toward the gate and I spotted a camera looking down at us. A sign on the wire fence surrounding the property read Property Protected by Bishop Security.

I looked over toward the other side of the fence, then turned to Alex. "You think I can make it over?"

Alex looked up toward the top of the fence. "If you do, you'll have about three minutes to get into the unit and get whatever it is that's inside."

"Maybe take it through that gate?" I looked back at my car, not the prettiest thing but not sure I was ready to destroy another car.

I walked around the perimeter of the fencing and looked in toward the storage units. The ones on the exterior—just inside the fence—were the ones with full-sized garage doors. I kept walking until I saw units numbered in the seventeen hundreds. "There it is, unit one-seven-eight-six."

I looked at the barbed-wire on top of the fence. Even if I could climb to the top—a challenge in my topsiders—I wasn't sure how I'd get anything heavy back over and outside the fence.

"Any ideas?" Alex said.

Rebel Storage wasn't one of the more modern storage facilities. In fact, the building looked a bit old, with rust stains coming down the sides over the faded, blue exterior walls. But it didn't matter—they clearly had security in place.

"I'll give it a try," I said. I reached up and stuck my hands through the wired fencing. I pulled myself up, slipped my foot inside and pulled myself higher. I moved fast once I was moving up the fence. Within a few seconds I was all the way up top.

But then it was the barbed wire I had to deal with.

I looked down at Alex.

She said, "You'll never get under that."

I held on to the horizontal rail and slid my arm just under the wire. There didn't seem to be enough space to get my body underneath. Not without ripping the barb through my skin. But I was already up there. I had to give it a try.

I got my leg up over the rail and tried to slip it under the wire. I thought for a second I'd make it through. But that's when I felt the tear.

Pain shot through my leg, like a fork had been stuck into my calf. Blood dripped down the wired fencing.

Alex said, "You're bleeding."

She wasn't telling me something I didn't know.

I looked down toward Alex. My hand slipped from the top rail and my body dropped. But I didn't hit the ground. Instead, my body slammed against the wired fence and bounced off. My leg was caught in the barbed wire. I hung upside down.

Alex reached up and tried to hold me from falling. She held me by my shoulders. But even though there were just a few feet to fall, as soon as my jeans—or my skin—ripped from the barbed wire I'd hit the ground harder than I'd like.

Alex was positioned under me when my jeans finally ripped, the weight of my body pulling me down toward the ground. I fell on top of Alex and we both hit the ground.

"Are you okay?" I said.

Alex looked dazed, not saying a word. Not until she looked down at my leg. "That doesn't look good."

There was blood inside the tear in my jeans. Blood that came from my torn skin. I looked up toward the top of the fence. "I was shocked. The barbed wire's electrified."

I pushed myself up to my feet and helped Alex from the ground. "Go stand over there," I said. "Near that brick wall."

"What are you doing?"

"Just get over there," I said. "Stay out of the way."

I pulled open the driver's side door of my car and stepped inside. I turned the key in the ignition but it didn't start. Not on the first try. I turned the key again and the engine turned over.

I turned the car around and drove away from the fence, maybe fifty or a hundred feet from the front entrance. I revved the engine and jammed the car into drive, my left foot on the brake, my right foot pushing the gas pedal down to the floor. The wheels engaged and the tires smoked until I popped my foot from the brake. I must've hit fifty miles an hour by the time I got to the fence as I turned the steering wheel just enough so I didn't hit the vertical poles head-on. Instead, I clipped the corner of the fencing. It peeled open like a banana.

Some of the poles ripped out of the ground and dangled from the wired fence that'd wrapped itself around the front of my car.

I stopped just inside the fence and stepped out of the car. I ran toward unit one-seven-eight-six and stuck the key in the lock.

Alex ducked inside the hole in the fence.

"Don't come in," I said. "Get in the car."

I slipped the key in the lock and lifted the garage door open. Inside was a red Lincoln Town Car with a white vinyl roof.

Alex watched me from the other side of the fence. "Is it locked?"

I opened the front driver-side door and reached for the ignition to see if there was a key. I pulled down the visor but there was nothing there. I lifted the floor mat on the driver's side and found a single key. I stepped out and stuck the key in the trunk's lock and lifted the lid. Over my shoulder I said, "Cops'll be here any minute."

Inside was a crate. It looked identical to the one at the Gem and Mineral Society.

I reached inside and tried to lift it. But it was too heavy.

Alex stepped in next to me and we both tried to lift it, but it wouldn't budge.

"How heavy could it be?" she said.

I shrugged. "At least a few hundred pounds. We'll never get it out of here." I heard sirens off in the distance. "Shit."

"What do we do?" Alex said.

"Get in my car. Drive it out of here. Meet me at the marina."
I slammed the trunk lid closed.

Alex stood still.

"Go on, Alex. Get out of here."

The sound of the sirens grew louder. Alex ran toward my car, jumped inside and turned over the engine on the first try. She backed the car out from the mangled fence as metal scraped against metal. The sound was ear-piercing.

I jumped into the front seat of the Town Car. The engine dragged, not wanting to start. It wouldn't turn over.

The sirens grew louder.

I turned the key again, slapped my foot down on the gas pedal and the engine came alive. I slammed the gas pedal down on the floor and slapped the shift on the steering wheel into reverse. My body lunged forward as the car yanked itself through the opening behind me. It scraped along the edge of the wall, took off the side view mirror and a good section of trim. I ripped the steering wheel hard to the left and spun the car around, faced the open fencing and drove through.

Sheriff's cruisers were now in sight as I hit the gas and drove straight over the grass, through a thick wall of green trees and bordering shrubs. I was unsure where I'd end up, but jumped a curb and drove straight out into the middle of the street.

There was an oncoming truck—the air horn blew at me—but I slammed my foot down on the pedal again. The rear end of the Town Car fishtailed until I straightened the wheel. I looked behind me, the grill of the tractor trailer truck was just inches from the trunk of the car.

Chapter 40

ALEX WAS WAITING FOR me by the fuel dock at Trout River Marina, just a few feet from where one of the Dock Hands, Jack Richards, tossed empty pallets onto a forklift.

Jack stopped and looked my way when I stepped out of the red Lincoln with the white roof.

"Hey Jack," I said with a nod.

He kept his gaze on me for a moment before he said, "I didn't know it was you driving that thing. How goes it?"

I shook his hand as he gripped mine hard, squeezed it like a vice.

"Any plans to move back here?" he said. "I know I speak for everyone when I say you're missed around here."

I smiled. "Appreciate that, Jack. But I don't know. Not sure I can swing the cost of a new boat."

"No insurance on your boat?"

I shook my head. "Actually, that wasn't my boat I was living on. I was taking care of it for a friend. He'd been living on it when it exploded." I looked out toward the St. Johns. "I do miss it."

Jack wiped the sweat from his brow with the back of his forearm. He reached down for another pallet and tossed it onto the forklift.

Jack was older—past sixty with gray creeping up the side of his head—but he was built like an ox. And from what he said, he'd never even stepped foot in a gym. He worked hard, that's all.

He looked down at my bloody jeans. "What happened to your leg?" he said.

I looked down. "Just a little mishap." I glanced back at Alex and again turned to Jack. "Jack, mind if I ask you a favor?"

He tossed another pallet onto the forklift. "Whatever you need."

With my thumb I pointed toward the Town Car. "Got a wooden crate in the back of that car, can't lift it myself."

Jack looked out toward the lot. "The Town Car? Is that yours?"

I shook my head. "Actually, no." I turned toward the Impala, the steel peeled off the frame on one side, the windshield one bump away from being shattered. "The Impala's mine. But the crate's inside the Lincoln."

Jack rubbed his chin. "I know they're all over the place, those older Lincolns, but I've seen that one around. Almost sure of it." He paused. "Late one night, recently, if I remember correctly. Might've been when I was coming out of the restaurant, likely a little after midnight."

Alex and I exchanged a look.

"You sure it was that car?" I said. "Any chance you saw who was driving it?"

He scratched his head. "Young kid. In fact, crossed my mind to call the sheriff's office." He straightened the baseball hat on his head. "See a young man in here late at night, driving around like that...they gotta be up to somethin', no?" He reached down and picked up another pallet.

I looked around the marina, over toward the dock where Philip's boat had been when the bomb exploded, some of the wood still charred from the fire.

Jack said, "Well, let me help you with that crate. I'm taking off in a bit."

We walked to the Lincoln and together pulled the crate from the trunk.

"Christ," he said as we both strained. "You're not kidding. This thing's heavy. What the hell is it?"

"I'm not exactly sure. Haven't had a chance to open it."

We carried it over to my car. Alex popped the trunk as Jack and I placed it inside.

I reached for Jack's hand. "Appreciate the help." I looked around the marina. "If you don't mind...if anybody asks, you never saw me here."

He gave me a nod and walked back toward the dock.

I moved the Lincoln to a space at the far end of the lot, around the corner of one of the buildings.

As soon as I stepped around the corner, two Sheriff's vehicles drove slowly into the lot. A spotlight shined along the parked cars as it moved toward the docks.

I stayed low and ran between a row of cars as I made my way toward Alex, waiting for me in my car.

The sirens chirped. One of the vehicles accelerated across the lot and stopped right at the dock where Jack was loading pallets. An officer stepped from his vehicle and stopped to talk to Jack.

I watched him shake his head and shrug his shoulders as I ducked into the passenger side of my car. "*Go!*" I said. "Get out of here..."

Alex put the car in drive and took off for the exit. I turned in my seat toward Jack and the officer as we left the marina, turned onto Trout River Drive headed for the Main Street Bridge.

My phone was still on the front seat when I picked it up for the first time since we were at Rebel Storage. I had the ringer off, as I usually did, and missed a handful of calls. Three of them were from Billy, all within the past half hour.

His message said to call him back. And that it was urgent.

I called him back and he answered on the first ring.

"She took off," Billy said.

"Who?"

"Kathleen. She's gone. I've been trying to reach you."

"Yeah, I was a little hung up," I said.

I glanced over at Alex as she rolled her eyes.

"I heard her on her phone out on my deck. She came back in and said she had to go. I don't know where she went...or who she was talking to..."

"Her husband?"

"I wish I knew, Henry."

"Kind of strange, isn't it?" I said.

"Very. And she was in a hurry."

"Did someone pick her up?"

"She jumped in a cab."

We were both quiet for a moment.

253

GREGORY PAYETTE

"Sorry, Henry. I tried to—"

"Forget it. It's not your fault. I just hope she's okay."

"I should've followed her."

"Don't sweat it." I hung up and looked over at Alex. "Kathleen took off."

Alex kept her eyes on the road, not showing much concern.

"You like this car, don't you," I said.

She laughed. "Yeah, it's a beauty."

The window was smashed on the passenger side, the fenders two different colors, and now missing much more paint than before. The rear bumper was held on with wire and duct tape, and the engine—I was sure—needed a complete rebuild. At least the radio worked.

"Maybe you were right about her," I said.

Alex said, "Do you know where she was staying?"

I shook my head. "The only time I asked, I got the feeling she didn't want me to know. Like she pretended she didn't hear me."

• • • ●• ● ● •• •

Alex and I were back at Billy's house, the three of us stood around the island in the middle of Billy's kitchen.

Billy said, "So this call you got...it wasn't from whoever gave Chloe that key?"

I shook my head. "I'm pretty sure it was Charles. But he's not who called me. Why would Charles give me a key, then have someone call me to deliver what's inside that crate?"

Alex and Billy both nodded in agreement.

Billy said, "Did you call him?"

254

"I left him a message. I was hoping he would've called back by now."

"What about the crate? Where is it now?" Billy said.

"In my trunk. Problem is, the damn thing's too heavy to lift. Had to have one of the deck hands over at the marina help me lift it. But I don't like having it in my trunk."

"Why don't you leave it here?" Billy said.

I shook my head. "I might need it to get Victoria back." My phone vibrated on top of the kitchen counter. I looked down at the screen and answered the call.

Before I said a word, the voice on the other end said, "Bring the sculpture to the Evergreen Cemetery at midnight tonight. Come alone. And you tell the cops...she's dead."

The call disconnected.

I looked at my watch and looked at Billy and Alex. "I have an hour."

Billy pulled an old .38 Special from a drawer in the island. "I'll go with you. I've been eager to use this...I just picked it up at an auction. And if whoever you're going to meet had something to do with blowing up my restaurant..."

"No," I said. "I can't take the chance. He said if anybody else comes with me...he'll kill her." I started toward the door.

But Alex grabbed me from behind.

"No way I'm letting you go alone. I'll go with you."

We looked each other in the eye.

"You can't," I said. I looked at Billy. "I'd love to have you both come. I'm sure it'll be fun, but..."

Alex wouldn't let go of my arm. "Just listen to me. I have an idea..."

Chapter 41

I TURNED RIGHT ONTO US-17, turned onto Winona and into an entrance to Evergreen Cemetery. I kept the car moving at a crawl, doing all I could to keep the engine quiet. But even at an idle it had a roar to it.

I was on Woodlawn and continued straight until I saw what looked like a brief flash off in the distance. I was sure it was headlights.

I continued past the live oaks covered in spanish moss and evergreens and gravestones and tall monuments. An interesting place, but I would've preferred the tour in daylight.

I came to an intersection and stopped, looked both ways and far ahead toward where I thought I saw the headlights flash. But I wasn't sure which direction to turn, so I decided to shut off the engine and wait.

My phone rang.

"Why'd you stop?" the voice said.

"Where are you?"

"Drive toward the light." The caller hung up and I immediately saw the lights flash again. I drove to the left with my headlights off.

I had no idea what I was walking—or driving—into. I'd already been shot. The boat and my car'd been blown up. And it's likely someone was hoping I was upstairs at Billy's when they blew the roof off his restaurant.

The odds seemed to be heavily stacked against me.

I leaned forward with my chin just over the steering wheel trying to get a better view of where I was going. Cemeteries were creepy enough, never mind in the pitch black on a cloudy night, when even the light from the moon wasn't enough.

Up ahead I saw a car facing in my direction.

I stopped, turned off my engine, and stepped outside. I gently pushed the door closed behind me, trying not to make much noise.

It was quiet.

Too quiet.

The click of a gun filled the air. I felt a cold muzzle pressed against the back of my skull.

"You'd better've come alone." Whoever it was stood behind me and ran his hand up the inside of my legs and around my ankles and waist.

I looked over my shoulder. "Dominic?"

He eased up on the gun pressed against my skull. "Open the trunk," he said.

"You're alive?"

"No, I'm a ghost."

"Where is she?"

"Open the trunk."

"I want to see Victoria first."

"Once I see inside the trunk." He flicked his wrist and motioned with the gun for me to move toward the rear of my car. "Go ahead," he said. "I don't have all night."

I pulled my key from my pocket and pretended to wiggle it in the trunk's lock. I pulled it out and held it up in the air. "You have a flashlight? I can't see. I'm not even sure it's the right key." I shrugged. "Just got the car...it's a fixer-upper, as you can see."

He pointed his gun at my head. "Open the goddamn trunk"

"I hope you didn't come alone. It weighs at least a few hundred pounds. Heavier than whatever it was you delivered to Julie."

"If I have to take your car, that's what I'll do."

"And leave yours here?" I squinted and looked toward his car. I could barely see it. "I'd say that's a fair trade."

Dominic pushed the muzzle hard into the back of my head. "Let's go. Open it *now*."

"So what exactly was the deal back there at the Gem and Mineral Society? Looked to me like you were dead. Good trick, whatever you did."

Dominic said, "I ask again, you won't be alive to ask another question."

I held up my hand and dangled the keys from my fingers. "I'm telling you, I don't know which key it is. Go ahead...you give it a try."

Dominic stared at me for a moment then grabbed the keys from my hand. With his gun still on me, he stepped around me and stood behind the trunk. He stuck the key in the lock.

The hood flew open faster and harder than he expected. Alex jumped out gripping her Glock with both hands, pointed right at Dominic's face. "Drop your gun, guido."

He started to raise his hands in the air. But he hadn't dropped his gun. It looked, for a moment, like he was thinking about his options.

I wasn't going to take the chance, so I threw myself at him and grabbed the arm holding the gun. I twisted it behind his back and flipped him over and slammed him down to the ground. As he started to come back up, I threw my knee under his chin.

Alex jumped out from the trunk with her gun pointed down toward him. She stood over him with her Glock pointed at his face. "Stay down!"

"Where's Victoria?" I said.

He wouldn't answer.

I grabbed a clump of his hair from the back of his head, my fist clenched tight. I lifted him to his feet and pulled his head back as I looked straight into his eyes. "Dominic, where is she?"

Alex grabbed Dominic's gun and handed it to me. I pushed the muzzle against the back of his head as Alex turned and started toward Dominic's car.

Dominic tried to look back at me. "You won't shoot me," he said. "I know all about you. You wouldn't shoot a..."

I lifted him just enough to drive my knee into his chest. He curled up in a ball as he dropped down to the ground. I held the gun with both hands and stood over him.

"Go ahead," he said through his clenched teeth. "Let's see if you have the balls to shoot me."

I moved the gun toward his foot, took aim, and pulled the trigger.

The shot rang out and echoed through the cemetery.

Dominic screamed in a way I didn't expect a man his size—or any man, really—would scream.

Alex turned and ran back toward me and screamed, "Henry?"

Dominic whimpered. "Crazy son of a bitch. He...he shot me."

I looked back at Alex and shrugged. "He dared me."

"Where'd you shoot him?"

"In the foot." I shrugged. "He'll live." I kept the gun on him, just in case.

Alex turned and headed back to Dominic's car.

"Be careful," I said.

She put her hand up over her head and gave me a wave without looking back. The closer she got to the other car the harder it was to see her. It couldn't have been any darker outside.

I said to Dominic, "Now we're even."

"What the hell's that supposed to mean?" He held his foot with both hands.

"Are you going to tell me it wasn't you out in Neptune Beach?"

He was quiet for a moment, aside from the whimpering. "I have no idea what you're talking about."

"No?" I waited a moment. "It was your car. You were there when I got shot, weren't you."

Dominic didn't answer. He tried to get up but I held the gun on him and pushed against the back of his head with my foot. "I think it's best you stay down there."

I heard Alex open the doors on Dominic's car. She yelled back to me. "There's nobody in the car."

"You check the trunk?"

Alex was quiet for a moment. A light brightened the area around the rear of the car when she popped the trunk.

"Empty," she said, loud enough for me to hear.

She started walking back toward us as lights came around the corner and across the grass between the Live Oaks, Spanish Moss hanging close to the ground, creating long shadows from what looked to be a van.

The engine roared as it drove straight for Alex.

She lifted her gun and took a shot at the van, but it raced toward her.

"Alex!" I yelled.

Dominic grabbed me by the leg and pulled me down to the ground. He pulled a gun from the back of his pants, but I kicked it from his hand. The van drove past Alex and headed right toward me and Dominic.

I moved as fast as I could out of the way and the van rammed right into the side of my car. It didn't budge far but went up on two wheels before it came crashing down and slammed to the ground.

A shot rang out and I was sure a bullet hit the ground just at my feet. I turned, ready to fire, but didn't know where Dominic had gone.

Another shot came my way and I turned to run.

Alex ran past me at full speed. "It's a trap," she said and continued past me into the collection of headstones and monuments.

Another shot was fired our way and a spark burst just in front of Alex where the bullet had struck a headstone.

We both ducked behind a monument. I glanced up and the face of the statue was looking down on me.

Alex pulled out her gun, taking aim toward my car where the van was stopped. More shots were fired our way.

I pushed her arm down and shook my head. "Don't."

"I had a shot," she said.

"We don't need to be in a shootout right now. Who knows how many there are." I stuck my head around the side of the base of the monument. But it was hard to see. The lights of the van were turned toward us. "Stay down," I said.

"We're just going to sit here?"

I turned to Alex but didn't say a word.

The van turned around and backed up to my car. Then I saw another set of headlights go on. Doors slammed and the sound of thin steel echoed around us.

The van's headlights moved as the van turned away and headed for the exit. Dominic's car followed as they raced over the hill. The tires squealed and stones spit out from under the wheels.

A moment later, they were gone.

I got up and walked toward my car. The doors were open except for the one on the driver's side. It was crushed deep into the interior of the car. Broken glass covered the seats. Steel was pushed in so far it blocked the steering wheel. There was no way I could drive the car.

I walked around to the open trunk and looked inside. I turned to Alex. "They have the pelican."

Chapter 42

I OPENED MY EYES, my head on a pillow that wasn't mine. Sun blasted through the blinds from a window across the room. I sat up, looked around, and realized I was at Billy's house. There were voices coming from down the hall.

I got up and walked into the kitchen where Billy and Alex stood at the island drinking tea and talking.

"Nobody thought to wake me up?" I said. I walked over to the coffee machine and poured myself a cup.

Alex said, "We thought you could use some rest."

I looked up at the clock on the wall above the stove. "Ten o'clock? Already" I couldn't believe it. "I haven't slept this late in years."

My phone buzzed on the counter. I picked it up and looked at the screen, but didn't recognize the number. I answered it anyway. "Walsh Investigations."

"Henry, hey, uh...it's Charles Weiss."

"Charles? Where have you been? I've been trying to reach you."

"Oh, right. Sorry." Charles was quiet for a moment. "We need to talk."

"Yeah, no kidding." I held the phone against my chest and said to Alex and Billy, "It's Charles." I asked Charles where he was.

"Neptune Beach," he said.

"With Carla?"

"Carla? Ha, no. I'm alone. Skip's Bar. Ever hear of it?"

I said, "I think you know I've been there."

Charles went quiet. Even though it was still morning, I could hear a crowd in the background.

"You get the package I dropped off for you?"

"I wasn't sure it was from you, but I assumed so."

"Did you get the..." He paused for a moment, then spoke into the phone in a hushed voice. "The pelican...was it in there?" I could hear Charles breathing into the phone, like his mouth was wrapped around the mouthpiece.

I looked over at Billy. "Can you give us a ride out to Neptune Beach?"

"How soon? I have a meeting."

"With who?"

Billy stared back at me but didn't answer. "You can take one of my cars." He turned to Alex. "Maybe you can drive. Or at least make sure he doesn't destroy this one."

• • • • ● • ● • • •

Alex and I sat down at the bar at Skip's. I looked around for Charles, but didn't see him anywhere.

Jackson stood at the far end of the bar with a cigarette in his hand. He looked up at the TV, then glanced along the bar and gave me a nod. He pushed out his cigarette in an ashtray and walked toward us.

He reached across the bar and shook my hand. "Henry," he said.

I was starting to feel at home in the place. "You remember Alex?" I said.

He nodded with a smile, his gaze held on her for a few seconds too long. "Hard to forget." He threw down two coasters. "What're you having?"

"I'll have a Jack," I said.

Jackson held up two fingers. "Two cubes, right?"

I nodded. "You'd be surprised how hard that is for some bartenders."

"Maybe the ones who don't drink whiskey," he said as he turned to Alex. "What'll you have?"

"Just a beer. I don't care what kind."

Jackson nodded and turned away.

"Jackson," I said, glancing around. "Any chance you've seen Charles Weiss in here today? I spoke to him no more than a half hour ago. He said he was here."

Jackson turned with our drinks and nodded, looking toward the far back corner of the place. "Over there. Been here quite a while."

I turned and saw what looked like the back of Charles's head just over the back of the red, vinyl booth.

I threw down a twenty. "Keep the change."

We walked up to the table where Charles sat alone. He faced the other direction with his eyes on a small TV on the wall.

"Hi Charles."

He seemed to be startled, but broke out a smile when he looked past me and gazed at Alex.

His face was a mess. His puffy eyes half closed...but I'd guessed that'd been the booze.

"Jesus," I said as I looked back at him, his face bruised and battered. "What happened?"

He gestured with his hand for us to sit down across from him. "Some bodyguard, huh?"

"Dominic?"

Charles nodded.

With a gentle touch he put his fingers on a purple bruise on his face. "He was with this kid. Beat the shit out of me."

"You know who?"

"Who the kid was?" Charles shook his head.

His left eye was swollen, almost closed shut. Besides the wound under his eye, he had a cut through the middle of his thin, white eyebrow. There was a lump right at his hairline at the top of his head, and what looked like dried blood on the edge of his right ear.

Alex and I sat down across from him.

"Was he looking for the pelican?"

Charles nodded. "Of course he was. But I didn't tell him a thing."

"You didn't tell him you'd dropped off the key for me?"

"The key to the storage facility?" He shook his head. "Why would I tell him that?"

I took a deep breath and looked over toward the bar. "Because he knew I was there."

He shook his head. "I'm telling you, I—"

"Why the hell'd you hire him in the first place?" I said.

Charles sipped from a martini glass and shrugged. "I needed a bodyguard."

"I can see that. But why him? Did you even know him?"

Charles shook his head. "Not at all. He showed up though, out of the blue. At the time, I figured it was just good timing."

"Good timing?"

"After some things that'd been happening...threats I'd received. Mostly, at the time, I think they were coming from Jeanpaul DePierre." Charles sipped his martini, holding his glass by the stem. "Jeanpaul's the artist who designed the sculpture. He's in France."

I nodded. "I know who he is. In fact, I had a brief conversation with him. And unless he's as good an actor as he is an artist, I don't believe he'd ever threatened you."

Charles said, "Why would I lie? I'm telling you, he threatened me."

"I'm not saying you're lying. But, if you're telling me Jeanpaul personally threatened you, then—"

"Well, no. Not directly. It was people that worked for him, I guess."

Alex and I exchanged a look. I leaned forward on the table. "Charles, don't you think it was something more than a coincidence Dominic showed up and offered to protect you right around the time you're getting threats from a man who, as far as I can tell, had no intention of causing you an ounce of harm?"

Charles straightened himself up in the booth across from me and Alex. He stared into his drink without saying a word.

"Jeanpaul was never after you, Charles. I spoke to him myself. Of course, there's a chance he's not being honest with me. Hard to know for sure from five thousand miles away."

Alex said, "Charles, if you didn't tell Dominic you'd dropped off those keys to Henry, then how'd he know he was getting the sculpture?"

Charles shrugged. "I have no idea. Really...I didn't tell him. I'm lucky he didn't kill me."

"Why didn't you go in there and get it yourself? Why bring me the key?"

"That's what I was told to do."

"By who?"

"Philip. He sent it to me, told me to get it to you...said if anybody could get it out, you could."

"But wasn't Philip the one who put it in there?"

Charles shook his head. "It was Frank. Frank let Philip know he'd found it."

I looked at Alex, and could tell she was having as much trouble pulling it all together as I was.

Charles held his glass in his hand and looked at me over the rim. "So you got it?"

I shook my head. "I had it. But it's gone. I was set up."

Charles put his drink down. The expression dropped from his face as he leaned forward on the table. "It's gone? What's that mean? Where is it?"

"Dominic has it."

"You sure?"

"That's just the thing. I'm not sure what you're not telling me. But he'd called me just as I got there. I didn't know it was him at the time. I mean, I had a good idea. And he said he had Victoria. So we met and—"

"You gave it to him? Are you saying you found Victoria?"

I stared back at Charles. "No. I had no intention of giving it to him. Not at first. And once we realized he didn't have Victoria—"

"Wait, wait, wait," Charles said as he rested his head down in his hand. "You're telling me you had it? You got it out of the storage facility? But now it's gone? The pelican...is gone?"

I glanced at Alex and said, "I'm going to get it back."

Charles shook his head. "Jesus, Henry. He's probably long gone by now. Who knows where it is." He looked down into his glass.

I said, "Do you have any idea where he would've gone?"

"Not at all. He never even told me where he lived. Said he was staying with a friend. But never told me who that friend was, either. I was always a little suspicious, I guess. Especially lately."

"What about your ex-wife?"

"Carla?"

I nodded. "Don't you remember? I told you...Carla delivered that crate to Julie. Dominic was with her."

Charles looked over toward the bar. He seemed to be thinking, and said, "Dominic has a wife, you know. I don't know who she is, but—"

"He's married?"

Charles pushed his glass aside. "To be honest I didn't know until, well..." He sipped his drink. "I heard him on the phone a few times. I could tell he was talking to a woman. If it's not his wife, then maybe a girlfriend? I just thought if you could find her..."

"You have a name? Or anything?"

Charles nodded. "I heard him call her Kate." He stared back at me for a moment, a slight nod to his head.

"Kate? Are you sure?"

Charles shrugged. "Pretty sure."

"And you think she might be around here?"

Charles finished the rest of his drink and slid his empty glass to the edge of the table. "He used to use the landline at the shop when he didn't think I was around. Not that it mattered, but he was sneaky with these calls. That area...doesn't have great cell reception. His cell never worked out there." He raised his empty glass a little off the table, trying to catch the waitress's eye. "That's when I started to wonder if he was playing straight with me." He pointed to the bruises on his face. "Guess I was onto something."

The waitress came over and put another martini down in front of Charles. He wiggled his finger back and forth toward me and Alex. "You want anything?"

We shook our heads and the waitress turned and walked away.

"Charles, where is she?"

"Oh, right." He held his glass by the stem, took a sip and put it back down in front of him. "My phone records showed a bunch of calls to a place called Riverside Inn."

I said, "That's where I saw Dominic with Carla."

He cocked his head. "Dominic and Carla were at Riverside Inn together?"

"When they first picked up that crate. We talked about this, didn't we? I told you."

I looked at Alex and she widened her eyes. looking back at me.

"I don't remember you mentioning the Inn," Charles said. "I knew Dominic and Carla did a couple of small jobs together. I guess I didn't think nothing of it."

Chapter 43

I PULLED ON THE front door to the Riverside Inn and let Alex walk in ahead of me. We both made our way toward the front desk.

There was an older woman behind the desk. She smiled and said, "Welcome to Riverside Inn. Are you—"

"Sorry, we're not staying." I looked around the place, decorated with older decor, dark wallpaper with big floral designs and a few old couches setup around a fireplace that wasn't lit. "I'm looking for Kathleen Valeriana."

She shifted her gaze to her computer screen and clicked on the keyboard in front of her. "Valeriana? With a V?"

I nodded. "Yes, with a V."

Alex stood by. "Her last name's Valeriana?"

The woman behind the desk opened her mouth to speak, but Alex tugged at my arm and gave a nod toward the stairs.

It was Kathleen, walking down the stairs with a travel bag over her shoulder. She stopped, mid-step, and looked right at me. "Henry?" she said. "What are you—"

"Kathleen Valeriana? Or do you prefer Kate? I would've never in a million years pictured you with someone like him."

Kathleen took a moment before she spoke. She took another step down. "I have no idea what you're talking about." She glanced toward the woman behind the desk.

Alex looked back and forth from me to Kathleen.

"It never registered with me how interested you were in Philip's business. Even when we first met, you wouldn't stop asking questions about him. You acted as if you had no idea who he was. But you knew exactly who he was. I remember the conversation you had with him... You talked about the rare gems and crystals and the sculpture he wouldn't mention by name. You knew exactly what it was." I huffed out a slight laugh. "And here I was, thinking it was me you were after."

Kathleen kept her gaze on me, but not saying a word.

Alex pulled her gun from the back of her waist and held it down by her side.

I said to Kathleen, "Philip told you all about that sculpture. He told you about the deal his father had made to get it. And what a big deal it was for his family to be in possession of such a valuable piece created by the famous artist from France." I thought for a moment. "At the time, it didn't mean a thing to me. I sat quietly with Victoria. I barely paid attention." I turned to Alex. "I had a lot to drink."

Kathleen stepped off the stairs, but remained quiet.

I turned to Alex and said, "I guess I should've listened to you." I looked back at Kathleen. "You knew about the pelican. Carla told Dominic about it. She knew him, didn't she."

Kathleen kept quiet.

"So you show up in Ocracoke looking for it. You saw me as a way to get to Philip, since he was already with Victoria. But the plans changed. And when you found out Philip and

273

Victoria were in Florida...you both came looking for it. And you thought I'd be foolish enough to lead you to it."

Kathleen squinted her eyes. "I guess you think you're pretty smart."

"It makes sense now," I said. "You went for Frank first. You got him to come after me, thinking he'd already been burned by Philip. He'd easily turn against his brother. But he changed his mind...so you killed him, too."

Kathleen said, "I didn't kill him. Not personally."

"I'm sure Dominic is quite capable of handling that," I said. "The same way he killed that young girl at Darcy Rental for no reason."

Alex raised her gun from her side and held it on Kathleen. "I could pop her right now."

"Where's Dominic?" I said. "Is he here?"

Kathleen turned and looked up the stairs, then shrugged. "I have no idea where he is."

"No? Just like you have no idea where Victoria is? Or who blew up Philip's boat?"

Kathleen looked past us, toward the front door, then toward another door off to the side of where she was standing.

"I know all about Jayray and his bomb making skills."

"We didn't want Philip killed. How would we've found the sculpture if he's dead?" Kathleen took a few steps sideways and moved toward the door just a few feet away from where she stood. She had one hand behind her back. "We always assumed Carla knew where it was."

"But she didn't have a clue," I said.

Kathleen shook her head. "We made her a deal."

"The diamonds?"

"If that's what you want to call them." She smiled.

"They're not even diamonds, are they?" I said.

Kathleen laughed. "Genuine cubic zirconia. The only person Carla could go to who would've known the difference was Julie Sanders. But we set her up before she had a chance to figure it out...got her out of the way."

"I'll be honest, I thought Charles set her up." I scratched my chin and thought for a moment. "So that kidnapping at the Gem and Mineral Society...it was all a set up?"

"Jayray was already working with us by then. Of course, Carla had no idea who I was and didn't ask. She certainly didn't know I was Dominic's wife."

"Kathleen, you have to tell us where Victoria is. Unless you want us to—"

Kathleen dropped her bag and moved her hand from behind her back. She held her arms out straight and pointed a gun straight at me and Alex.

Alex didn't budge, her Glock still on Kathleen. "There are at least six officers waiting for you outside," she said. "They're expecting us to come out with you. But if for some reason we don't..."

I was in the line of fire. I lifted my arms up on either side of me, one hand out toward Alex, the other toward Kathleen. "Can we wait a minute here with the guns?" I looked at Kathleen. "You have what you want, assuming you know where Dominic is? Just tell me where Victoria is. That's all I care about."

Kathleen and Alex held steady, neither one putting down their gun.

"Kathleen, please," I said. "Just tell me where she is."

I looked past Kathleen. Over her shoulder I saw Jayray come down the stairs. He had a semi-automatic rifle in his hands.

I said, "I guess you like the big toys, huh Jayray?"

He stepped slowly down the stairs and stood next to Kathleen. They both turned and looked back as Dominic turned the corner.

He had a gun pointed at the head of Philip's fiancé, Victoria. Tears ran down her cheeks.

"Victoria?" I said. "Don't worry, you'll be okay." I glanced at Alex and nodded toward Dominic. "You have what you want. Let Victoria go."

He shook his head. "We get out of here without being followed by your friends out there, then we'll see...maybe we'll let her go."

"What'd you do with Philip?"

Jayray spoke up. "He's putting some 'shrimp on the barbie'."

"What the hell was that?" Dominic said as he stared down the stairs at Jayray.

"Sorry, that's my Australian accent. Not bad, though, right?"

Dominic let out a breath and shook his head as he looked toward Kathleen. "I've had enough of this kid, you know."

I took a step back and stood beside Alex. "Victoria, Philip flew out to Sydney. He told me you'd called him..."

She nodded. "They made me call him. I told him that's where I was, that he had to fly out there right away."

Kathleen smiled and glanced back at Victoria. "She was really quite convincing."

Dominic moved down the stairs, the muzzle of his gun still against the side of Kathleen's head. He gripped her arm with his free hand and guided her down each step then stood next to Kathleen.

I said to Dominic. "Where's the pelican?"

He looked toward the door and said, "You ask a lot of stupid questions, Walsh. You really think I'm going to tell you?" Dominic had a limp in his step as he moved toward the door.

I turned and glanced at the woman behind the desk, visibly shaken, her eyes glossed over with tears. Both of her hands were down behind the desk, and she was somewhat hunched, leaning down.

She gave me a subtle nod...and I hoped I knew what she meant. I looked on the wall behind her and saw a framed photo of an older gentleman. I couldn't quite make out what was etched on a gold plate underneath, but it appeared to be a birthdate followed by an end date.

Her husband, I wondered.

I nodded back at her, knowing we had a small window. As I looked across the faces of Kathleen and Dominic and Jayray and Victoria I turned and lunged at Alex, bringing her down to the floor and out of the line of fire.

It was the old woman behind the desk who came up with what appeared to be a 12-gauge shotgun. It kicked up on her as she fired, missing all humans—probably a good thing considering the mess it would've made—but instead blew a hole the size of a softball through the wall just over Dominic's shoulder.

The sound that followed was pure silence, my ears ringing inside my head as I watched from the floor.

Alex came up firing and hit Dominic somewhere in the upper body.

He let go of Victoria as he grasped his chest and stumbled backwards, one step after the other. His foot caught the bottom step. He reached for Victoria to catch his fall but she pushed his hand away and ran up the stairs away from him.

Dominic laid on the floor. Blood soaked through his shirt.

Jayray ran past Kathleen and knocked her down.

She got up on her feet and followed Jayray toward the door. But the door swung closed on her as she tried to get away. She stumbled backwards and fell to the floor.

Alex didn't waste a second as she jumped toward Kathleen and kicked the gun from Kathleen's hand.

Alex lifted her shirt, pulled a small thirty-eight from her waistband and tossed it in the air to me. I moved toward Dominic and I stood over him with the gun pointed right at his face.

But his eyes were closed. He wasn't going anywhere.

Chapter 44

WE WALKED THE PROPERTY along the St. Johns River where Billy's Place once stood. Billy held open the blueprints and showed us his plans for the new restaurant. "The vibe'll be a bit different. New menu...more music. And I know Henry can't wait for the dancing."

"I'm all for music," I said. "As long as it's good. But the dancing?" I gave him a look. "You'll ruin the place."

Alex said, "Everybody loved what you had. But I guess change can be a good thing." She turned and looked toward the river.

"I do like the idea of the outside bar," I said.

Billy said, "Makes me nervous, having two bars to worry about."

"Chloe's not going anywhere, is she?"

Billy shrugged. "You never know. It doesn't help that she has to go work somewhere else for the next six months. Or however long it'll take to rebuild."

I bent down and from the pile of rubble and debris picked up a piece of the old mirror Billy'd kept on the wall behind the bar. "I gotta say, if this is what it took to take down that mirror, then..."

Billy laughed just as my phone rang.

I put my finger up. "Sorry, give me a minute." I stepped away and answered. "Walsh Investigations."

"Henry? It's Philip. How are you, my friend?"

"Philip! Good to hear from you. I'm doing okay, I think. We're at Billy's Place, checking out the plans for his new restaurant."

"I hope Billy can forgive me."

"Are you kidding? I know he still feels a little strange using the money you sent him."

"It's the least I can do."

"And Jayray's looking at, I don't know, maybe fifty years on all counts."

"Yeah?"

"I don't know. That's what I hear."

"So where are you living?" Philip said.

"Might end up out at Neptune Beach. Carla's old place."

He went quiet for a moment.

"Did you get my package?"

"I did. It was more than I was expecting, but—"

"It was worth every penny, Henry."

I looked back at Alex and Billy talking with Chloe and her boyfriend Jake. They walked toward the St. Johns. I followed them, but hung a little behind as I talked with Philip.

"Have you talked to Charles?" I said.

"Yes, and he's been taken care of, finally. He's going back to Paris. In fact, he said he'll be seeing Jeanpaul, maybe even staying with him until he finds a place. Jeanpaul's happy, too.

You know, he's an interesting man. Said he just wanted to make sure whoever ended up with the pelican appreciated his art for the work he put into it." He paused for a moment. "The man would live on the streets if he had to...as long as he's doing what he loved. You should meet him. Reminds me of you, in some ways."

I didn't respond, although I guess maybe I knew what he meant.

"I still have a hard time believing it was Kathleen," I said.

"You know, I remember all the questions she asked me. We all had quite a bit to drink that night. If I hadn't opened my mouth about the sculpture, none of this would've happened."

"She had it all planned out, Philip. I was her target, knowing I was staying at your house." I looked back toward Alex and caught her looking my way. She smiled. "If I could learn to be a little more selective about the women I hang around with..."

"She was an attractive woman, Henry. Smart and interesting. Too bad she was a crook."

"Alex saw through her the moment she met her."

"Well, you know how she feels about you, don't you?"

"Alex?"

Philip laughed. "Yes, Henry. Who do you think I mean? I don't know what it is with you, someone like her right before your eyes...Ah, who am I to tell you what to do."

I glanced at Alex as her hair blew in the breeze. She stood on the dock next to Billy, smiling and laughing.

"Okay Philip, I'll let you go. Thanks for calling."

"Thank you again, Henry. Hopefully Victoria and I will celebrate our wedding one day soon. Once all the dust clears. But it'll be here in Sydney. So you'll have to fly for the wedding."

"Yeah, well, we'll see. I can always catch a boat."

I hung up and walked back over toward the dock. My closest friends were all together as we stood on the dock and looked up toward where the old Billy's Place used to stand...where the next one would be built.

"That was Philip?" Billy said.

I nodded.

Alex said, "Is everything okay?"

"Seems to be," I said.

Billy handed me a beer from a cooler and we all raised our drinks in a toast.

Alex leaned into me and smiled. "If you need a place to stay, the spare bedroom's all yours."

• • • • ● • ● • • •

Thank you for reading *The Crystal Pelican*. The series continues in *The Night the Music Died*. You can learn more about it and the other books in the Henry Walsh series by visiting my website:

www.GregoryPayette.com

Sign up for the newsletter on my website:

GregoryPayette.com

Once or twice a month I'll send you updates and news. Plus, you'll be the first to hear about new releases with special prices. If you'd like to receive the Henry Walsh prequel (for free) use the sign-up form here: **GregoryPayette.com/crossroad**

Also by Gregory Payette
Visit GregoryPayette.com for the complete catalog:
HENRY WALSH MYSTERIES
Dead at Third
The Last Ride
The Crystal Pelican
The Night the Music Died
Dead Men Don't Smile
Dead in the Creek
Dropped Dead
Dead Luck
JOE SHELDON SERIES
Play It Cool
Play It Again
Play It Down
U.S. MARSHAL CHARLIE HARLOW
Shake the Trees
Trackdown
JAKE HORN MYSTERIES
Murder at Morrissey Motel
STANDALONES
Biscayne Boogie
Tell Them I'm Dead
Drag the Man Down
Half Cocked
Danny Womack's .38